Don't Get Caught

By Ater Imber

ISBN: 978-1520320540

Published in Canada

Published by Ater Imber
contact@aterimber.com
http://aterimber.com/

This is a collected work of fictional stories. Stories and situations are entirely the product of the author's imagination and characters are based upon original fictional characters created by Erik Kripke for the t.v. series Supernatural. Any resemblance to actual persons, living or dead, is entirely coincidental.

For Miss Ruth Moniz - the best English teacher I ever had. If you ever see this, I hope you know I couldn't have done this without you pushing me to write less.

For Mandy - who I've always carried with me in my heart. I wish you were here to see this.

And for Blonday - if it wasn't for you, this wouldn't have happened.

Table of Contents

Sunday Blues

"Go! Have fun!"

"What if I don't like fun?"

"Really? *That's* the excuse you're going with?"

His roommate gave him the most skeptical look he'd ever seen in his life--he would've laughed if he was in a better mood. He let out a long sigh before dragging himself vertical with reluctance to walk to the door. The giant sitting on the edge of the couch threw him the keys and couldn't hide the shit-eating grin that appeared on his face--one way or another, they both knew he'd end up going.

Stupid Sam... I don't even drink *coffee!* Dean walked toward the little café that was on campus. The only time he'd ever been in there was once to pick up some soy something or other for Sam when he was running late.

A waiter tapped him on the shoulder, *What the..?* Lost in thought, Dean hadn't even realized he was sitting in the café already.

"What can I get for you?" The barista tapped his pen against his notepad.

"I don't know--whaddaya got?" Dean searched the table for a menu.

"You've never been in a café before, have you?" He shot back, smirking down at the blonde-haired customer.

Dean had to give him credit; he didn't seem as completely douche-y as he'd originally thought. Still though, how often does one get the chance to have some fun with customer service reps?

"Listen buddy, I don't know where that passes for good customer service, but I'd like to order without the snark, m'kay?" Dean folded his arms over his chest and raised an eyebrow at the blue-eyed man.

"Are you gonna tell me your order or are you waiting for a personalized invitation?" He cracked his gum and placed a hand on his hip without missing a beat.

"I'd like to speak to your manager," he glared up at the apron-clad shorty.

The barista let out a loud sigh before rolling his eyes and walking away.

Dick, Dean watched him disappear behind a swinging door.

Outside the window next to him, it started to rain, *Oh great. Now I'm gonna be stuck in here with that guy until it stops.*

"Excuse me?" A female voice grabbed Dean's attention.

He drew his eyes up the body of a pretty little blonde thing standing at the end of his table, "Look, before you launch into whatever speech you've been trying to construct for the past ten minutes, let me cut you the nervousness. I'm flattered, really, but I'm not in the mood, all right?" Dismissive, Dean rubbed at his eyes.

The girl turned bright red before hurrying away. Dean watched her go before turning his attention back out to the view out the window. Or lack of one. The rain was coming down so hard he couldn't see--the only visible thing was a wall of water running down the glass.

"Sir?"

Dean looked up to see the barista staring at him expectantly again.

"Apparently, you assumed the manager was going to flirt with you, so she felt it'd be better if you talked with the owner."

"Awesome," he rubbed his hands together in anticipation. "Sooo where is he?" Dean looked around.

"I'm sorry. My bad. I never did introduce myself, did I?"

Oh c'mon! Dean thought as the waiter--ahem, *owner*-- extended his hand.

"Cas, and it's a *pleasure* to meet you..?"

Dean hesitated, eyeing the black-haired coffee jockey and then accepted the outstretched hand, "Dean," he grumbled.

"Well *Dean*, can I offer you our house special? A big plate of manners with a side order of not being a dick?" He offered with a smirk, placing one hand on his hip and loudly cracking his gum.

"I'm gonna go out on a limb here and say that you wouldn't accept an *'I'm sorry'* from me, would you?" A sheepish smile crept across his full lips.

"Tell you what. You order something you think we actually carry and I'll call it even," Cas bargained, giving him a wink before sashaying away again.

Did that really just happen? Dean eyed Cas's retreating form, while pulling his phone from his pocket.

"Sam," Dean lowered his voice, mindful of the sudden stares from the other tables. "What the hell do café's serve?" Sam was laughing hysterically on the other end of the phone, "Dude! Stop laughing. This isn't funny! What kind of restaurant doesn't have menus?"

"Sorry dude, you're on your own for this one," Sam broke the connection.

"Oh well, that wasn't helpful." Dean rolled his eyes before flipping the phone closed.

"You figure something out yet?" Cas' voice made Dean jump.

Shit.

"Umm… A-a coffee?" He stuttered out, feeling his cheeks grow red.

Cas chuckled and nodded, pulling his notepad out of his apron pocket.

"That's a start. What kind of coffee, hotshot?" Cas smirked.

"Black, jack-ass." Dean countered smugly, crossing his arms and leaning back in his chair.

"Is that really any way to talk to the person who's about to handle your food?" Cas shot back.

Fuck. The man winked again before he swished away, leaving a surprised Dean in his wake.

He's actually got a pretty nice… Nope, no way! I am not *goin' there!* He shook his head and forced himself to stare out the window and very pointedly *not* at the man--*owner's*--ass.

Dean let out a sigh and closed his eyes, working to focus on the sound of the rain. It was actually working pretty well--he'd managed to tune out all the café background noise. The hard part now was allowing his mind to wander everywhere except to the waiter (god-damn, *owner*) and how not hot he was.

He wasn't going to let himself think about how clean and crisp his uniform looked, or how straight he stood up. Or about the way his whole body leaned back slightly when he'd laughed. Definitely wasn't thinking about how neat his writing had been, or that he was left-handed or had an indent where he held

the pen on his middle finger.

Wasn't at all thinking about how clear the colour of his eyes were--they were almost the colour of blue fire--or about the crow's feet he had in the corners of them, or the way they crinkled when he smiled. And he was most definitely *not* thinking about his perfectly tossed bed-head that looked half-intentional.

Fuck.

Dean opened his eyes to find the man of the hour standing in front of him with an eyebrow raised in concern-- his order on the table between them.

"Why're you looking at me like that?" Dean asked, fighting the urge to rub at his eyes and swallowed down the yawn creeping up his throat.

"Some of the other customers were complaining about the noises you were making in your sleep." Cas plopped himself down in the chair opposite of him.

"Really? That's weird considering I wasn't sleeping."

Cas rolled his eyes and crossed his arms, "Oh please. You turned this place into a lumber yard for an hour. Chased tonnes of customers out."

"If it was such an inconvenience, why didn't you wake me up and kick me out?" Dean looked around, noticing the place was empty.

Shit.

"H-how long have I been sitting here?"

"About three hours."

Cas jumped up and patted his back before he even realized he was coughing. "I-I'm okay." Dean sputtered after a couple of minutes.

"All right, good," Cas nodded, rubbing circles into his back.

God, that feels good… Dean unconsciously leaned into the touch.

He couldn't tell you how long they stayed standing there with him rubbing circles into his back, but they both jumped when the door bell chimed, signalling a customer.

"Hey! I was just wondering if you'd seen… Dean!" Sam caught sight of the two men at the table and walked over.

"You know each other?" Cas asked.

Dean looked up at him in surprise, *Was that disappointment?*

"Yeah, he's the crazy roommate I've been telling you so much about," Sam smiled at the aforementioned pain-in-the-ass.

"I'm not *that* bad to deal with."

Everything was always easier when Sam was there. He seemed to have the same effect on Dean that a couple drinks usually did--relaxing him. And now Cas, too... But that didn't make any sense. They just met five minutes ago, *Um, three hours, Dip-shit.* Every time Cas came back to the table, all he could think about was how not to look like a dumb-ass. What the hell was that? Why was he so worried about looking stupid?

Yeah, that didn't add up.

"Dean's right Sam, other than chasing away a few customers, he's actually not that hard to take." Cas said, throwing a wink in the blonde's direction.

"He chased out customers? What was he doing?" Sam eyed his roommate with concern, wondering what trouble he would need to get him out of this time.

"I didn't do anything! I just kind of... dozed off." Dean crossed his arms across his chest in a huff.

"Well, I guess that explains where you've been for *three hours*," Sam smirked.

"Do you want your usual Sam? On the house if you get the lumberjack over here to leave." Cas pushed playfully at Dean.

"Yeah, sure. That sounds great."

Both roommates were silent for a moment as they watched Cas walk across the café and disappear into the kitchen.

"You are so stupid!" Sam smacked the other man on the arm.

"Um, ow!"

"Cas was flirting with you, you idiot!" Sam smacked him again.

"Pfft, dude, *please*." Dean rolled his eyes.

"No, trust me Dean. He was."

"Is that so? And how do you know?" Dean leaned back and crossed his arms.

"Well, you've been here for three hours, didn't buy anything, *and* he didn't kick you out."

"I *did* buy something," he gestured to the cup of coffee on the table.

"Did you pay yet?"

Dean paused. "Nooo..."

"I repeat. Didn't buy anything." Sam gave him Bitch Face Forty-Seven.

"I was going to pay when I left," Dean shot back in his best pouty five-year-old sneer.

Sam looked down into the cup, "You didn't even drink it."

"I was asleep." Dean shrugged.

"Again... Here for that long, *chased out customers,* and he still didn't kick you out."

"It was raining?" Dean arched an eyebrow.

"He kept coming over to talk to you."

"He was my waiter, Sam. He was just doing his job."

"Why were you the only customer he was talking to..?"

"This place was pretty dead when I got here. Not many other customers to take care of." Sam just wasn't going to leave it alone.

"He was rubbing your back when I got here, man."

"I had been choking. It was a medical intervention. Would you rather the guy let me choke to death?"

"And then he winked at you," Sam crossed his arms.

"That? Okay, I can't explain."

"Ha! I'm telling you dude, the guy-"

"One no fat, mocha soy latte, no foam, extra whip, with chocolate chips, caramel drizzle and shaved dark chocolate on top with a glow-in-the-dark curly straw!" Cas's assistant called out from the kitchen window, hitting the bell and sliding the drink onto the ledge.

"Jesus, can you believe some of these pretentious coffee hut nerds?" Dean shook his head and shot a look at Sam.

"Yeah, nerds…" Sam's cheeks turned red.

"C'mon guys, don't make me say it again!" The cook yelled, hitting the bell several times again with impatience.

"What a douche bag. First, the guy orders *that* and then he doesn't even have the decency to *not* make them wait?" Dean shook his head again.

Sam chuckled nervously and shifted his weight to his other leg, slipping his hands into his pockets. Dean looked over at him curiously, raising an eyebrow.

"You okay?"

"Whoever this order is better get over here right now before I add an extra ingredient!" The cook's voice bellowed from behind the counter while the bell from the window sailed out to shatter on the ground.

There was a moment of silence, the few other customers looking around trying to find out whose it was.

"What a douche bag," Dean mumbled, slipping his hands in his pockets and looking at the ground.

Sam ducked his head and wished that his face wasn't still as red as he thought it was.

"That's it!" Luce the cook yelled through the order window, taking the top off the drink and holding it up to his mouth.

"Whoa! Luce calm down!" Cas shouted as he came out of a back room.

Luce jumped a little at the sudden voice, spilling some of the drink down his shirt and glared at Cas. Reluctantly, he put the cap back on the drink and set it down.

Cas walked over and whispered something fiercely to the him. The cook continued to glare at the owner, but nodded before he disappeared away from the delivery window. Cas picked up the drink, took the lid back off and seemed to inspect it.

After a minute or so he nodded to himself, put the lid back on and walked over to where the two roommates were still standing.

"You're not hard of hearing are you Sam?" Cas placed his order down on the table.

"What?" Sam responded, tearing his eyes away from the order window and down to the black haired man.

"I'll take that as a yes," Cas smiled, patting the giant's arm.

"Sorry," Sam mumbled, making a point not to look at the shocked expression on his roommate's face.

"No need to apologize to me, it's Luce you should go apologize to. He doesn't like when people don't pick up their orders," Cas said with a tight smile.

"Yeah, I got that."

Sam looked back to the window and saw the cook there, glaring directly at him. Sam shifted his gaze away in a hurry, not wanting to further upset the firecracker who was only a wall away.

"I think we should go now before you do something else to piss him off," Dean suggested, standing back up.

"That's a good idea," Cas nodded, looking between the two men.

"Sorry that we messed up your shop so much," Sam apologized, a sheepish look on his face.

"It's fine, you didn't mess it up that bad. I can undo the damage," Cas swatted him playfully.

"Looks like he likes you," Dean teased as they passed the kitchen and noticed the cook still glaring at him.

"Shut up," Sam mumbled under his breath as he hurried through the door.

"Hey," Cas stopped Dean with a soft hand on his arm, "we're having a karaoke night tonight at eight. Think you can come?"

"Uh, yeah sure." Dean blushed, a crooked grin tugging at the corner of his mouth.

"Okay cool!" Cas beamed, and bounced back toward the kitchen. "See you soon."

Dean watched his ass as he left and had to force himself not to bite his lip.

Yes you will.

Beer Patrol

"**H**ey," Dean grinned as he came around the corner, balancing a beer and two plates of pizza. "Hey," you smiled back, sitting up and swinging your feet out of the way to make room for him on the couch next to you.

He side-stepped the coffee table and handed you a plate before plopping himself down where your feet had been. You gave a pointed look to the beer in his hand and raised an eyebrow as he stuffed a pizza slice into his face. Feeling the weight of your stare, he cautiously looked in your direction, his easy body language disappearing.

He stopped chewing, a wad of pizza bulging out one of his cheeks. He spoke around the mouthful, "What?"

"Beer?" You took a small bite of your own slice, but held his eyes.

Appearing confused, his eyes darted to the beverage in question before shifting back to you, still looking for the answer. He chewed slowly while he thought, the confusion wrinkling his forehead.

"You get one and I don't?" Your tone slightly icy.

He swallowed the pizza down hard and looked back and forth between you and the bottle again. He dropped his head a bit while a tinge of red swept across his cheeks. He cleared his throat.

"D-"

"You don't have one," the words came out fast, cutting you off, "because you're not old enough to drink."

That was not the answer you were expecting and your back stiffened in surprise. The quick words stung and though you tried to hide it, the discomfort worked its way into your expression.

Dean glanced away, uncharacteristically shy for a moment before looking back to you and he grew concerned when he took in your own expression. Absorbing the look on your face, he calculated what he'd done wrong, "C'mon, what?" The words much softer than the previous explanation.

Swallowing down your pride, "It's fine Dean, I just… didn't think that would be a rule you'd abide by," you could feel your own cheeks heating up. No way you could sit there in front of him while it happened. It was stupid and embarrassing. Putting your food down in a hurry, you attempted to make a graceful escape from the room, but he was talking again.

"Of course I *abide* by that rule. I don't want you to end up lying in some ditch off the side of a road, because I gave you a beer." When you tried to brush by him, Dean grabbed hold of your arm to keep you from leaving.

Though you tried twisting your wrist free while the blush continued to creep up your cheeks, he wouldn't let you. The hand on your arm was firm and he wasn't having any of it. You stopped pulling away, "Y-you don't?" You stuttered, feeling your heart start to hammer against your chest.

Dean was taken aback, the disbelief very evident, "Of course not. How could you think I'd want you to die?" He asked incredulously.

You felt the hot sting of tears in your eyes at the surprised face in front of you. Why was his mind always one extreme or the other? Too many years hunting monsters had taught him to view every situation as black or white, life or death. But sometimes a beer was just a beer and not necessarily the set-up for vehicular manslaughter. What could you do with a guy like that?

"I don't! I just-" You cut yourself off and turned away just as you felt the tears start their traitorous descent down your face. It was only a beer, but the rest of it was too big. With Dean in it, everything around what your life had become was big. It made the little things, the *normal* things, all out of whack. It was difficult to deal with any of those things like regular people anymore.

"Whoa, hey, don't cry. C'mere," putting his food down, he pulled you into his chest, wrapping his arms protectively around you.

You stayed stiff with embarrassment a second and then let yourself go, safe in his arms and felt only somewhat guilty that your tears were soaking through his shirt.

He murmured into your hair, "Let's get this straight, okay? I will do whatever it takes to keep you safe," his voice was softened by his concern and he rocked you slightly as he held you.

You allowed yourself to cry, if possible, harder with those words. You never knew that Mr. More-Whiskey-Than-Blood-Winchester would be so concerned about your alcohol intake. It wasn't that you were surprised he cared so much, it was just with everything else he let you do--hunt, stitch him up, *drive*--you never thought that he'd draw the line for inappropriate things for you to do at drinking. Besides that, you were one-hundred-and-thirty-percent sure he'd had many of his own beers before he was in a legal position to do it.

You knew it was stupid and didn't make any sense--why were you so irrational sometimes? "I'm wrecking your shirt," you sniffed after a moment, working to collect yourself.

Maybe my period's coming...

"It's just a shirt," he said into your hair as he hugged you tighter.

"It's your best shirt."

"No, *you're* my best shirt," Dean countered with a smile in his voice.

"That doesn't make sense," you chuckled, sitting back up and wiping at your eyes.

"Yes, it does."

"How?"

"You are the best thing I've ever had covering my chest," he said with a soft smile.

"That's by far the sappiest thing you've ever said," you laughed. How did he always manage to do that? Say exactly the right thing at exactly the right moment. When it mattered.

"Oh? Okay, how about this instead... Shut up and eat your damn pizza." The words were an order, but the tone that carried them conveyed something else entirely. With a quick examination to be sure you really were fine, he stood from the couch and aimed for the hall.

"Where are you going?"

"I'm going to pee. Is that all right with you?" He turned back around and crossed his arms over his chest with a look of mock expectation on his face.

"No," you said with a laugh.

"Too bad," he turned on his heal and headed down the hall to the bathroom, raising a hand over his shoulder to flip you off behind him as he left the room.

"I love you, too."

Unable

"You boys ready to order?" The blonde, skinny waitress smiled down at the two in the booth, pen poised against the top of her notepad.

"I'll have the blueberry pancakes and a black coffee, please," the younger of the two replied, smiling back at her.

"Sure thing, Hun. And you?" She turned to face the older man.

"Make that two coffees and a cheeseburger," he said with a smile, closing his menu as he looked the girl up and down.

"Oh, I'm sorry, we don't have burgers." The waitress, Nancy it said on her nametag, sighed softly in exasperation and kept the tight customer-friendly smile pasted in place.

"Oh, right, sorry." Dean shifted in his seat and flipping the menu back open, looked it over again.

"No need to apologize, I know there's millions of joints like us that do. Guess the management here never got the memo," Nancy replied with a shrug.

"I'll have the, uh… apple pie," he declared after some deliberation, snapping the menu closed again.

"We don't sell pie before four." Nancy's smile faded into confusion.

The man looked down at his menu again, clearing his throat. A blush crept up his face.

"Soup?" He asked hopefully, looking up from under his lids.

"We only serve soup at night." Nancy's annoyance was becoming obvious.

"Sandwich then?" The blonde man asked in a barely audible voice.

"Can you order something that's actually *on* the menu, please?" Nancy tapped her foot with impatience.

"O-of course, sorry." Head still down, his eyes frantically searched the menu.

"Tell you what. How about you actually read the menu and I'll come back," Nancy suggested tersely before walking away.

He threw his menu down on the table and leaned back in his seat, running a hand down his face. For once, his eyes didn't follow the waitresses retreating backside and instead, were fixed on the tabletop.

"Dean, what the hell?" The younger man asked leaning across the table, confused. "Seriously."

"Sam, don't," the clipped reply matched his face. Dean looked really pissed-off.

Sam looked him over with concern, "Are you okay, man?"

"Yeah, I'm freakin' awesome," Dean rolled his eyes. "Leave it, okay?"

"Dude, I'm serious. "Sam lowered his voice as a few people walked in, "Why didn't you just order something they have?"

"Let it go Sam," Dean hissed, leaning closer. He looked out sideways across the Greasy Spoon and then back at the other man. "Just leave it alone."

"Wait." Sam straightened back up, eyes widening in understanding.

"Sam-"

"Can't you-?" His eyes narrowed, "Did you forget how to read, Dean?" Sam hissed at his brother in surprise.

"No, I didn't *forget*," he scoffed with a half-hearted laugh. "Seriously, dude, let it go already." Fidgety, Dean slid a hand inside his open jacket and adjusted his ivory-gripped pistol.

"But…" Sam knew his brother well. Despite the hard crusty coating, there was more going on underneath. He narrowed his eyes in concentration, thinking. "Dean…" His eyes flicked to the closed menu and back at his brother's face. *No, that's crazy…* His forehead furrowed. "Can't you… read? I mean, at all?" He asked incredulously, even as the words came out of his mouth thinking what a ridiculous question it was.

"Of course I can read, Sam! I'm not an idiot," Dean's face went red.

"Then why didn't you just order off the menu?" Sam countered, crossing his arms.

"Jesus, Sam. We're not having this discussion," Dean mumbled.

"Yes, we are. How can you not read?" Sam pointed toward a word on his menu, "Do you know these letters?"

"Of course, I know the letters! I know the freakin' alphabet, College Boy." Dean hissed, slapping the menu out of his face.

"I don't understand. You fill out forms all the time."

"Shut up, Sam."

"Dean, but that means you don't know how to write, either."

"Shut *up*, Sam."

"How did you never learn? We went to school."

Dean slammed his fist down on the table and stood up, shaking in anger. The noise caused some other patrons to turn around.

"I'm leaving." Without another look in Sam's direction, his jaw clenched, Dean hurried out the door.

Throwing some money onto the tabletop for the food he'd ordered, Sam stood up and followed right behind him, muttering a contrite 'sorry' to the other people in the diner. Dean wretched the driver side door open and got in, slamming it with a huff, just as Sam reached the car.

Dean threw the Impala into gear, but before he got the passenger door open, his brother stomped on the gas and screeched away. "Dean, hang on a minute!" Sam called out behind the car as Dean drove off.

Eyes on the retreating car, Sam continued to work on making sense of the shocking revelation, *How did I never notice before?*

*****

Sam got the key out of his pocket to unlock the door of the motel room, glad to see the Impala was in the parking lot. That meant Dean didn't need to blow off any steam at a bar. Hearing muffled conversation, he paused before sliding the key into the lock and pressed his ear to the door. It wasn't clear enough through the door, so he crept around the side of the motel to their open window and saw Cas holding Dean in his arms on the edge of one of the beds.

Maybe he did go get drunk.

"Dean, I'm sure you're being completely irrational about this. I doubt that Sam would intentionally embarrass you." Cas brought one of his hands up to run through Dean's hair.

"You weren't there. You should've heard him, Cas. It would've been less embarrassing if he up hung a banner that said 'Dean Winchester can't read'." Dean's voice was shaking.

"I'm sure that's not true," Cas said softly, his face a mask of concern that appeared out of place over his normally expressionless features.

Dean didn't reply. He sniffed loudly and Cas brought him closer to his chest.

What the hell is going on? Sam's eyes widening as he continued to watch. He felt a bit guilty for spying, but he couldn't seem to turn away.

"It's nothing to be embarrassed about, Dean. Illiteracy is a growing problem," Cas said, changing tactics.

"Easy for you to say. A six-year-old knows how to read. I'm stupider then a freakin' *six year old!*" Bursting out of the embrace, Dean pulled himself up to the headboard of the bed, opting to lean against it.

Cas followed him up, positioning himself beside Dean. They were sitting close enough for their shoulders to touch, but Cas pushed Dean's head onto his chest and held him close.

"Dean, it's okay." Cas placed a gentle kiss on the top of Dean's head.

Holy-shit-holy-shit-holy-shit! Sam hurried back over to the door, jammed the key in the lock, and burst into the room.

Cas and Dean jumped apart, both with furious blushes on their faces. They avoided Sam's eyes while they got it under control in a hurry.

Sam dragged a confused hand through his hair, "What the hell just happened?" His mind was racing, not really willing to accept the reality of what he'd just seen, though the evidence seemed to speak for itself.

The other two men flashed a look at each other before looking back at Sam, both their expressions now carefully blank.

"What do you mean?"

"Oh, don't give me that crap, Dean! You know what I mean! The cuddling and the-the-the comforting. And the freaking *kiss!*" Sam took a charged step closer, causing both men to take a hurried step back.

"Dean was upset and yes, I comforted him. It is my understanding that humans do that in these types of situations." Cas stated in his usual, non-emotional way.

"Oh, no! *No!*" Sam pointed an accusatory finger in Cas's direction, "You don't get to try and pull that angelic I-don't-understand-human-nature-no-emotion crap after what I just saw!" Sam yelled at the angel, his mind still racing.

"Sam, why don't you just calm down and we can talk about this," Dean eyed his brother with caution. He'd been such a dick back at the restaurant and now he had the nerve to act like this? He wasn't the one who was publicly humiliated.

"Calm down? How the hell do you expect me to calm down when I just saw you get kissed by an angel?" Sam roared, turning his gaze on his brother.

"Sam, we can explain. If you would just sit down..." Cas said, gesturing to the bed.

"Explain? You two better have a really great-" Sam cut himself off, eyes growing wide and he looked from Dean to Cas' faces with a careful expression now.

"How long?" His voice was small and he refused to look either of them in the eye.

"How long what?"

"How long have you two been... You know..." Sam gestured from one to the other.

"Jesus, Sammy, I'm not *sleeping* with the guy!" Dean's face contorted in fake disgust.

"Then what the hell, Dean?"

"Technically, that would be what the heaven," Cas interjected.

The brothers looked to the angel for a moment before shaking their heads and turning back to face each other.

"Like I said, I can explain," Dean repeated, gruffly.

"I'd love to hear this." Sam crossed his arms as he sat down on the edge of the other bed.

"Okay well..." Dean trailed off, gesturing openly with his hand, trying to think of a way to explain it without sounding insane.

Sam raised an eyebrow at his brother in expectation, watching as he opened and closed his mouth a few times, as though he was unable to come up with a believable lie. Sam turned to look at the angel in the room who was starring at the floor like it was the most interesting thing on the planet in that moment.

"Yeah, Dean, that was a great explanation," Sam said sarcastically, rolling his eyes and huffing out a breath.

"You won't believe me," Dean snapped. "I'm trying to think of a way to tell you without sounding crazy, okay?"

"After everything we've been through, you could tell me anything and it wouldn't be crazy."

"Fine." He hesitated for a beat. "Cas has been helping me learn how to read and write for over a month now, but I'm not making any fucking progress." He paced a bit in agitation. "He comforts me like that, because… Well, because he read somewhere that that's how to comfort a 'struggling child'," Dean used his fingers to put quotes around the words.

Sam regarded his brother for a moment, his face frozen in a half-smirk. He looked over to the angel who nodded, confirming the story and walked up to stand beside the hunter.

"Well?" Dean prompted.

"That's crazy," Sam concluded standing up.

"I knew you'd say that," Dean grumbled, shifting toward the opposite wall. His posture stiff, his hands balled into fists at his sides.

"Dean, now's not the time," Cas's voice was calm and he reached out to place a soothing hand on his tense shoulder.

Dean took a deep breath and let it out slowly before turning back to his brother, his fists unclenching and his poster visibly relaxing.

I don't fucking believe this. Sam couldn't make it compute. The more he continued to watch the pair in front of him, the more his brain short-circuited.

"You expect me to believe that Cas is training you? Like some sort of puppy? Sam paused, hurt evident in his eyes. "Do you really think I'm that stupid?"

"No I don't think you're stupid, Mr. Pre-Law." Dean crossed his arms over his chest.

"What does that even mean?" Sam asked, confused.

Dean looked at him with a smile and shrug--he didn't know what it was supposed to mean, either.

"Well, what the hell, Dean? How have you never learned how to read? We went to school together. What were you doing instead of learning?" Sam worked to wrap his brain around everything that'd happened.

"You really want me to answer that Sammy?" Dean replied, his cocky smirk making an appearance.

"How do you fill out the forms for credit card fraud and stuff if you can't read or write?" Sam asked instead, hoping to get an actual answer out of his brother.

"Well, Sammy, it ain't rocket science. I watched Dad fill out the forms a thousand times. I know what shapes to put down where." Dean explained, blushing again and looking down at his boots.

Shapes? Then he clued-in. Sam's eyebrows disappeared into his hair. "You mean, you memorized the sheets?" Sam took a slight, unintentional step backwards.

"Like a map." Dean rubbed a hand over the back of his neck.

"Fuck…" Sam breathed out, looking at his brother with new found respect, his earlier suspicions vanishing.

"Actually, Dean has made remarkable progress these past weeks despite his earlier claim," Cas added, with a quick look in Dean's direction.

"Well., that's… That's just great." Maybe it really had all been innocent? Maybe too many years at his brother's side had taught him to be suspicious of every thing and every one. Or maybe, he just needed some air. He sighed and tried to pull it together.

"I-I need some air." Sam headed toward the door. He banged it shut behind him and headed for the parking lot.

"That was close." Dean said after Sam disappeared.

"Really close," the angel took the hunter's hand in his own.

"We need to be more careful," Dean said with seriousness, pulling the angel toward him and wrapping him up in his arms.

"Are you sure he's not ready for the truth?"

"Yeah I'm sure. You saw how he reacted before. He's definitely not ready," Dean was nodding.

The angel stepped away, going to look out the window. He worked to hide his hurt expression from the taller man. "I don't like hiding Dean."

"Whoa, hey... I thought we went over this," Dean went over to stand behind the black-haired man.

"We did, it's just... It feels like you don't want him to know. That you're ashamed of me," Cas confessed, dropping his head.

"Ashamed of you? Are you kidding? I'm not ashamed of you. You're the best thing I've got. Hell, if it were up to me, I'd run around town shouting my love for you from the rooftops and spray-painting it across every wall." Dean wrapped his arms around the angel from behind and leaned his head on his shoulder. "I just don't want to tell Sam if he's not going to take it well."

"What if he's never ready?" Cas's voice was quiet, but it was a large question.

A long silence spun out between them before Dean replied. "How 'bout this... We tell him in time for our anniversary. Okay?" Dean planted a kiss on the angel's forehead.

"Dean, that's six months away!"

"Exactly. It'll give him plenty of time to think of a gift." Dean smiled, spinning the angel around to face him.

"Is that all you can think about?" Cas chuckled.

"It's cleaner than what I was thinking before," he replied with a wink.

Cas leaned into him, "Is it now?"

"Oh yeah," he was nodding. "If Sam could read my mind,? The jig would've been up way before." He dipped his head and captured the angel's lips in his own.

*****

I don't believe this! Sam paced away from the motel, thinking over everything he'd been told.

How could I not know my brother couldn't read? Sam stuffed his hands into his front pants pockets and kicked a rock around the parking lot.

Okay, no. This actually makes sense, Thinking back over all the times he'd watched his brother fill out forms or sign his name when they checked into a new motel, he was always so focussed on what he wrote. Probably, because he was concentrating so hard. *How could I have not noticed that sooner?* No wonder he always left it up to Sam to do the research. It all made sense now.

He stopped short, *I am such an asshole. I shouldn't have left.*

"Damn it!" In sudden decision, he started back to the motel room.

He must have been so scared to tell me… I can't believe I just walked out. Good job, Sam. He kicked the rock along in front of him, taking his frustration out on the stone rather than something breakable.

Okay, but what the hell do I say now? 'Hey Dean, I'm sorry I walked out on you, let's fix this together?' That was stupid. He was never going to believe that.

Well, I need to start somewhere. Pausing outside the window, he looked inside in time to see his brother with his arms wrapped around the angel.

Oh my God... Sam took a few steps closer in morbid fascination, making sure to stay out of view.

He watched them laugh and then his brother, Dean-the-ladies-man-fucking-*Winchester*, spun the angel around to face him before giving Cas the biggest, romantic-movie kiss he'd ever seen in his life.

I fucking knew it!

The Impossible

"**C**as, c'mon man. You gotta know I didn't mean it," Dean sighed, running his hands through his hair as he prayed to the angel. It wasn't just any fight. Not this time. This time, it was serious--a major blow-out of celestial proportions and it didn't look like Cas was coming back. This was bad, and the hot-and-cold realization crept over him that their breaking up was a real possibility. If only he hadn't gotten so freakin' defensive--he thought he was helping protect him.

Dean looked around and felt the disappointment settle further into his stomach as the angel was nowhere to be seen. Since he flashed out, all Dean had done was pray to him, hoping to get him back.

"Cas, c'mon man, come back so we talk," Dean flopped down on the couch and scrubbed his hands over his face.

I just can't be around you right now

Cas's calloused response hit him hard, *Fuck! Cas, buddy, c'mon-*

Dean, no.

The hunter breathed out a sigh of exasperation and turned his head skyward. What the fuck was he supposed to do with the rest of his day?

Maybe I could go visit Sammy, see what he's up to. Dean idly twirled his thumbs around, *Yeah... I'll go see what Sam's up to.*

With that, the eldest hopped off the couch and headed for the door. Maybe seeing what his brother was doing would be more than enough time for Cas to decide to come back.

*****

"You like that, don't you?" Sam teased, trailing his fingers slowly down Gabriel's chest, pulling a beautiful moan from his lips.

"Sam, please," the angel gasped, bucking his hips against the hunters other hand, trying hard to get the friction he wanted.

"Ah-ah, be patient my angel," Sam cooed, smirking down at his captive.

"Fuck," Gabriel breathed as the giant's hand ghosted over the tip of his leaking cock.

"Sam?"

"Fuck!" Dean was calling from downstairs, killing the mood.

The hunter swirled around the room in a hurry, dancing around while gathering his clothes, hoping his brother would have enough sense to stay downstairs.

"Sam?" Dean called again, his voice at the bottom of the stairs.

"Hang on!" Sam called, pulling his shirt over his head and moving toward the door.

"Sam… Aren't you going to untie me?" Gabriel was straining against his bonds.

The giant looked back at his boyfriend and smirked.

"Nah, I'm good."

*****

"Dean!" Sam pounded down the stairs, "What're you doing here?" His brother was waiting on the couch.

"Not much. Just felt like seeing what you were up to," Dean stood up to hug his brother.

He better not notice my boner, Sam leaned in and wrapped his arms around his brother. But not too close.

"So… where's Gabriel?" Dean let the youngest go after a couple of beats.

I'm up here! Waiting for Sammy to come back and finish me…

Sam's face grew red at the intrusion.

"Sammy? You okay?" Dean eyed him with curiosity.

"Yeah, I-I'm fine." Sam hoped to Chuck that his face wasn't as red as he thought it was.

Saaammm-yyy… I can't wait until you get back so I can get your cock all nice and wet with my mouth. You know I know how you like it, right Sammy? Long, firm licks, coming up from the base all the way up to the tip…

"So…?" Dean looked at his brother expectedly.

"So…?" Sam parroted, wishing that Gabriel would just shut up.

Then, I'll suck up the sides of your cock slowly before slurping you into my mouth.

"So, where's Gabriel?" Dean repeated.

And, after I get you all hard and veiny for me, I'll smack your dick all over my lips, kiss it gently on the tip and dip my tongue just under the skin, getting a taste of your delicious pre-cum.

"Yo, dude. Hello?" Dean snapped his fingers in front of his brother's face when he didn't answer. "How many conversations are you having?"

"Oh, what? Uh, none. I mean, just one. With you. Yeah." Sam leaned himself against the banister and crossed a leg over his crotch to hide his hard-on.

"Sooo… Where's Gabriel?"

Sam shifted uncomfortably, "Gabriel's, uh, out. G-getting groceries?"

"Y'sure?" Dean gave him a sideways look.

"What? Yeah. *Yes*, of course I'm sure. He's definitely out getting groceries."

"Okay. Then why are you acting so weird?"

Because he doesn't want you to know I'm tied-up here naked... waiting for him to come back, so he can fuck *me nice and hard.*

"N-no reason," Sam scrubbed a hand across the back of his neck.

"Riiight..." Dean looked away at nothing in particular, his thoughts elsewhere.

Sammy... come fuck me, baby... I need to feel you deep *inside me...*

"So yeah," Sam coughed, "that's all we're, uh, up to."

That's not the only thing that's up, Sammich. Don't lie to your brother...

"Great."

"Yep."

"Oookay."

Both brothers shuffled in unease, neither coming up with anything meaningful to say while the uncomfortable silence stretched out between them.

"So, uh, shouldn't you be getting back to Cas?" Sam asked in a rush, crossing his arms over his chest, trying his best to block out Gabriel's teasing thoughts.

"Oh, right. I, uh, I should get back." Dean didn't appear in a hurry to leave. He flicked a look at the door and then back at his brother while he continued to linger, but Sam was already turning to show him out.

Why the hell is this so awkward? What was he just doing? Dean stared at his brother's back in concern as he led them to the door.

"Well, this was, uh... *fun*." Sam said with a tight grin, opening the door for his brother.

"Yeahhh...not the word I'd use," Dean replied with an awkward chuckle.

"So, we'll see you later?"

"Uh… sure. Just make sure both you and Gabriel come by.."

"Sure, sounds good," Sam fake-smiled and closed the door behind his brother.

"Gabriel!" Sam bellowed as he tore up the stairs.

Oh, shit.

Sam burst through the bedroom door, hungrily eyeing the man tied to the bed.

"You think that was funny?" Sam's voice was low as he stalked closer to the edge of the bed, ripping his shirt back off.

"Thought what was funny?" Gabriel asked innocently.

"Don't lie to me," Sam threatened, trailing his finger up his leg, smiling as the angel got goose bumps.

That action was rewarded with the angel's eyes fluttering and he arched his back into the touch.

"Na-ah, my angel, remember what I told you. *Patience*." Sam continued to tease him, as he came up the left side of the bed, his fingertips ghosting over his shaft again.

"Please, don't tease me," Gabriel begged, his voice taking on a frantic undertone.

"No, no. I'm going to make you pay *big* for that," Sam smirked, jerking the tip of his cock twice before letting it go and continuing up his body.

The angel breathed out a sigh of frustration and made a pouty face up at the hunter, hoping it would prompt him to speed things up. Sam got down on his hands and knees right beside his head and pressed a gentle kiss to his cheek, loving the moan that escaped the other's lips. He continued slowly kissing his way down to his neck, stopping a while to suck a hickey into the tender flesh.

"S-Sam..," Gabriel breathed, eyes fluttering closed as the sensation washed over him.

"Shhh..," the hunter cooed, gently rolling the angel's head, so he could suck the other side of his neck. This elicited another moan from the creature writhing in front of him, which just egged the taller man on more.

"That's right…" Sam breathed, cool breath tickling the hairs on the trapped man's ear.

"Sammy, *please.*" He was begging now, an undertone of urgency lacing his voice.

"No-no my angel… I'm going to make you pay for that."

*****

"Cas?" Dean called as he got back to his house.

"Yeah, I'm here." The angel sounded grumpy.

"Look, I'm sorry about what I said, okay? I was stupid and-"

"No, Dean." He stopped him. "*I'm* sorry." Standing up, he hugged the hunter to his chest.

You are? Dean allowed himself to be wrapped up.

"I am. It's all my fault. I see you were only trying to protect me and I shouldn't have got mad." He let go of the hunter before sitting back down.

"Uh… okay," Dean mumbled in surprise, sitting down himself.

"Can I ask where that came from?"

"What do you mean?" Cas asked, confused.

"Well, that's not how our fights usually end. What changed your mind?" For once, Cas let him off the hook without busting his chops. His heart melted.

"I had popped over to speak with Gabriel and he was in… a compromising position." Cas recalled with a look of confusion and disturbance.

"What kind of compromising position?" Dean wondered if that was the reason he hadn't been around when he visited Sam.

"It'd be best for me not to give you that mental picture," the angel didn't elaborate more than a small smile.

"Okay, so then we're good?"

"We're good," he confirmed with a nod.

"Just like that?" Dean raised an eyebrow at his angel.

"It was brought to my attention by my oh-so-helpful brother that it would be very stupid of me to let you go," Cas confessed to the floor, so he didn't have to meet his hunter's eyes.

"Well *that* is just obvious," Dean smirked.

Cas shook his head and kept his eyes on the ground, trying to hide his smile, *How could I have lived without you?*

Complications

"Will you?" Luce asked again, trying not to jump to the worst conclusion.

Sam just continued to stand there, an unreadable expression on his face. At first, Luce thought it was cute, how dazed into silence he was when the blonde got down on one knee and popped the question. But now, ten minutes later, with still no answer from him, he was worried--not only were his legs starting to hurt, but the patrons in the restaurant around them were starting to whisper.

Oh great… now I'm sweating. Luce wished he couldn't feel the slow trickle of sweat trail down his neck. He was working hard to keep his growing nervousness from being obvious to the crowd, but it was getting harder by the moment to keep it up, *Why isn't he saying anything? C'mon… Don't leave me hanging here…*

Luce shifted his arms slightly. His shoulders were starting to cramp from where they were still raised holding up the ring. *Why did I worry about getting such a big rock,* He turned his pleading eyes up to the giant in front of him.

"I'm sorry." Sam mumbled finally.

And then ran out of the restaurant.

Luce felt his heart shatter at the brunette's words. Things had been going so well, he had been so sure he'd say yes. How could he have been so stupid?

Luce picked himself up off the ground and placed the ring back in his pocket while unsuccessfully avoiding the pitied gazes of the other customers, *There go my plans for the rest of my day... life. Fuck...* Walking back over to their booth, he slumped down in his seat.

"I'm guessing you no longer need the champagne?" The owner placed a consoling hand on his shoulder.

Luce barely nodded, his eyes pinned to a dent in the table.

"Feel free to order whatever you want. It'll be on the house," the owner offered before scurrying away.

"Thanks," Luce said in a small voice and picked absently at the dent.

He sat there in silence, feeling numb all over. He just couldn't figure out why Sam had said no. They'd been on what Luce thought was Cloud 9 for months. Hell, he'd even hinted at getting married and the giant hadn't given any indication that he'd reject. He'd actually seemed ecstatic about the notion.

That was *a while ago though...* Luce thought back to the past couple weeks. Sam had seemed a bit more distant than usual, but when asked about what was wrong, he would say it was nothing. Just stress. Prying out of him what had him so stressed was pointless, because he refused to share. Luce chuckled humourlessly--proposing was supposed to surprise Sam out of his slump and make him forget about whatever he was so worried about. It was supposed to be a good thing.

Guess I was wrong... He took a sip of his water. *But why were* you *so worried?*

*****

"Damn, you're good." Gabriel panted, watching Sam run around the room, pulling his clothes on.

"I know," the giant winked, pulling his shirt over his head.

"You sure you can't stay longer?" Gabriel pouted.

"I can't, I told you. I'm meeting Luce." Sam hopped up and down as he struggled into his pants.

"I could make some of my famous chocolate chip pancakes," Gabriel said in a sing-song voice while wiggling his eyebrows hoping to entice him.

"I can't. I'm already late. I don't want to be late *and* dump him in the same night. That's just uber-douchey," Sam turned to face the small man in the bed.

Gabriel gave him his best pout and smiled as the hazel-eyed man sighed. Sam crawled back up the bed, wrapping his arms around his naked lover.

"Does it *have* to be tonight?" Gabriel asked after a moment of silence.

"Yes. I don't want to keep lying to him." Sam sighed, "And I don't like being a cheater." He squeezed the man in his arms tighter.

"Sammich, how many times do I need to tell you? It's not cheating because you haven't been having sex."

"Somehow, I don't think he'll share your view." After a pause, Sam released him and rolled himself off the bed.

"I'll miss you," Gabriel whined, following him to the door.

"I'll only be gone a few hours."

"Still. I don't like sharing," Gabriel grumbled.

"Look at it this way. After this, you'll never have to share me again. I'll be able to stay for so many pancakes you'll get sick of making them." Sam turned at the doorway as Gabriel leaned into him.

"Pffft, not likely," Gabriel wrapped his arms around the giant's middle again, pulling him in for another hug.

"Okay-okay. I *really* have to go now," Sam gave him a quick peck and worked to detach himself.

"Sammich?" Gabriel asked as he swung the door open.
"Yeah?"

"Don't be so worried. What could go wrong?"

A Thousand Promises

Sam lay awake in his bed, too excited to sleep. He rolled over and watched the love of his life snore away as if it were just any other night. That didn't surprise him--the trouble-maker could sleep through anything. Once, they went to a rock concert for Sam's birthday--after Gabriel's question of 'what do you mean you've never been to a concert?' had cemented them going--and halfway through it, Sam had asked him something only to find he was snoring away as if he were at home.

Sam never understood how the ball of energy was always falling asleep at the drop of a hat. Movies, sure, the giant understood falling asleep there--it's dark and the chairs are comfortable--but a *concert*?

I guess some things will just always be a mystery, he sighed, rolling onto his back to stare at the ceiling.

He knew that for tomorrow to arrive faster he should really be sleeping--no one wants to look tired on their wedding day--but he just couldn't seem to calm down enough to rest. His eyes wandered lazily over the familiar outline of the room--the pictures of them together, the dresser, and then there was his suit hanging on the closet door handle.

He couldn't wait to wear it. Gabriel was going to go nuts over it. He'd been careful not to put it out until after he'd fallen asleep to ensure he wouldn't sneak a peek. Sam's eyes ran over his fiancée's sleeping form with a smile. He couldn't seem to quell the butterflies that were working themselves up from his stomach and made him tingle all over when he thought of seeing his face light up when he walked in with it on.

*****

"Sammich!"

The six-year-old's head shot up, half-fearful eyes searching for the source of the voice. He finally spotted the mop of hair bouncing towards him and groaned, *Why does he always call me that?* It's not like he hated Gabe, the kid was just super annoying. He was always getting into trouble trying to be funny and Sam didn't understand where this newfound fascination with him had come from or why. They were practically from different planets--Sam paid attention and did his work and listened to the teacher and Gabe just.... *didn't.*

"Hey, Sammy! Why didn't you sit next to me on the bus?" Gabe pulled a lollipop out of his mouth with a slurp to inspect it.

"I guess I didn't see you," Sam didn't look up from his colouring. Maybe if he didn't make eye contact, he'd go away.

"You didn't *see* me?" Gabe's head snapped up and he lost his grip on the slobbery lollipop stick, "Awww, man..." It hit the ground with a wet smack. "Grrr... That was my favourite flavour in the whole world!" Gabe pouted and dragged a chair over, "Big dope. I was waving my arms around like this," demonstrating by waving his arms wildly above his head.

San shrugged, "It's not my fault you're short," trying to hold back a laugh at how stupid he looked.

Gabe flopped his arms back down and plopped himself down in the chair next to Sam, clearly not through bothering him. He hated playtime. It wasn't fair. They said to play *however* they wanted, but he always got in trouble for 'being too noisy' or 'being too violent'. They were stupid rules. You shouldn't tell people to do whatever they wanted if you were just going to yell at them later for doing it, *Grown-ups…*

That's why he invented a new game. He was going to get Sam to be his friend.

Sam was the best-behaved--and most boring--kid in the class. It would be fun to see how the teacher would react seeing the best and worst kids in class hanging out together. He was a weirdo, though. The kid almost never spoke, *Seriously weird. He's got like, no friends. Besides the kids who ask him stuff, 'cause of his big, stupid brain. But he never goes to their house. Or plays with them. Or* anything. *He always just sits there in the corner and colours. The whole time!*

Sooo weird… Gabe took it upon himself to teach Sam how to use his playtime effectively. And he knew he was actually helping out the teacher with Sam. He'd overheard her talking about his 'under-developed social skills' when he 'went to the bathroom' during library. He figured if he could help Sam be more outgoing or at least give him a friend, it'd help get the teacher off his back.

He looked around at the other kids, all of them in groups of two's or three's talking excitedly or laughing really loud--and then there was him and Sam, sitting in silence. He shook his head and watched him colour. That just wasn't what playtime was for.

"Do you want to play with me?" Gabe wiggled his eyebrows.

"No."

"Why not?"

"Because you'll get me in trouble."

"You don't know that," Gabe pouted and crossed his arms over his chest.

"Uh, yeah, you will."

"Shows what you know," Gabe stuck out his tongue and stuffed crayons into his pants' pockets. "We only get in trouble if we get caught."

*****

Cas consulted his clipboard, *Room... two-thirty, two-thirty, two-thirty... Wait, they're both in room two-thirty?* Hesitating in front of the closed elevator doors, he peered down the halls to his left and right, eyes narrowed. *This can't be right...* Cas growled in frustration, "I don't have time for this, people!"

"Call front desk extension, Baret Hotel," he enunciated carefully for the talk-to-dial and a moment later connected with the front desk clerk.

"I'm the wedding planner for the Winchester Wedding party. I'm looking for the room of one of the guests in our party. The *groom*, actually. I have noted that his partner, Sam Winchester, is in room two-thirty. But the groom's room is *also* two-thirty? This wasn't for the *honeymoon*, they weren't supposed to be in the same room."

The front desk clerk looked up the information while he waited on hold with growing impatience. Gabriel had said it was an emergency and he needed to hurry, *Oh-Em-Gee... Did he just put me on hold? Didn't I just say I was the wedding planner? If this glorified secretarial school drop-out delays the ceremony with his incompetence, I swear to Liza Minnelli I'll dump a bottle of Egalite on that snow white Persian carpet in the lounge as a permanent reminder not to mess with the clipboard!*

The desk clerk came back on the line. *Did I say Egalite? Psh, no-no-no, he's not worth wasting a bottle of good sparkling wine on. I'll use Merlot. Those bitches will never get that stain out.* Cas smirked in mental triumph and looked up at the wall on either side of the elevator, nodding his head as the desk clerk explained the hotel layout, "I see them," and noted the brass signs with the names of the wings of the hotel. "I see… Horizon and Morning Star. Wait, the room numbers are the same in either wing?"

Cas rolled his eyes, "If I might make a suggestion, honey? If you want your future guests to find their way around your establishment, you may want to rethink your naming convention so anyone with a rudimentary reading comprehension can find their own way around." He severed the connection with a huff, "The smartest thing that ever came out of that boy's mouth was probably a penis."

With a glance back up at the directional signs, Cas ran down the Horizon Wing to the end suite.

"What's the big emergency?" Cas burst into the room.

"I can't tie this friggin' tie!" Gabriel tugged at it in frustration.

"That's it?" Cas raised an eyebrow, but went to help him anyway.

"Yeah, that's it! Was this thing designed by NASA or something?" Gabriel grumbled.

"Stop, you're making it worse," Cas slapped his hands out of the way. "What in the name of Barbra Streisand did you do to this thing? How could you have known *me* this long and not know how to properly tie a tie?"

"Sammy's been doing my ties since prom," Gabriel confessed with a blush.

Cas chuckled and shook his head, "Of course, he has."

*****

"Sammich!"

Sam's head whipped up at the sound and he bounded down the stairs half-dressed, almost beating Dean to the door.

"Whoa! Where's the fire?" Dean leaned all his weight against the door before Sam could open it.

Sam groaned, "Dean, c'mon!" He worked to get around his older brother to pull it open with no luck.

"Why're you in such a hurry? You're not even dressed."

"We're getting ready *together*," Sam explained with a huff.

"Oh, I'm sure you are," Dean winked.

"Ew, Dean! Gross!"

"Guess you've still got a few more years for that to be embarrassing… Unless tonight's the big night…" Dean laughed suggestively.

"Dean!" Sam grunted, tugging on the door handle again. "Let him in!"

"Tonight's the big night for what?" John came around the corner into the front hall to see what the boys were fighting about. This time.

"Oh great…" Sam rolled his eyes.

"Dean, let the kid in, it's freezing outside," John glowered at his eldest.

Dean took his time moving off the door and sauntered over to stand beside his father. Sam wrenched the door open and had it closed again with Gabriel squished to his chest in the same instant.

"Whoa, Sammy. You miss me or something?" Gabriel hugged him back.

"I haven't seen you all semester!" Sam squished him closer.

"I know, I missed you, too."

"You're cold." Sam nuzzled his head into his chest.

"It's cold outside," he replied with a chuckle.

"Aw, aren't they adorable?" Dean broke in, smiling as the teenagers jumped apart.

The look of embarrassment on Sam's face seemed satisfactory enough for him, because he just winked again before leaving.

"Why don't you two go finish getting ready?" John suggested, much to Sam's relief.

Sam nodded shyly and dragged Gabriel up the stairs two at a time, not letting go of him until they were in his room with the door closed.

"Damn, Sam, you're sure eager," Gabriel plopped himself down on his bed.

"No. I just don't want you to have to endure my family," Sam shrugged off the comment and grabbed his blazer off the doorknob.

"I'm sure they're not that bad."

"Oh trust me. They're that bad."

"All right, I suppose you know them better."

"Yep."

Gabriel watched Sam continue to get ready in mild fascination. For someone who always seemed so well-organized, he rushed around his room throwing clothes everywhere like every other person Gabriel had met, himself included, *I guess as long as he looks okay at the end, it doesn't matter.* Sam was standing in front of the mirror picking at strands of his hair.

"Are you ready?" Sam's eyes flicked up to look at his reflection in the mirror.

"Yeah." Gabriel stood up and gave him a twirl.

"You don't have your tie on." Sam frowned, turning around to examine him better.

"Oh, right well... I just figured I already looked awesome without it. Putting it on wouldn't be fair to the other kids," Gabriel rubbed a guilty hand across the back of his neck and avoided Sam's eyes.

"Gabriel..."

"Fine! Fine. I, uh... don't know how to tie it." Gabriel pinned his gaze to the floor.

46

"What?"

"I just, I don't know. I'm not really the fanciest dresser. It's never come up before," Gabriel crossed his arms over his chest.

"Do you have it?" Sam went to Gabriel's rescue.

Gabriel nodded and took the crumbled piece of fabric out of his pants pocket, holding it up in shame. Sam took it delicately and flicked it, somehow getting the wrinkles out before throwing it around his neck and beginning to tie it.

"How do *you* know how to tie one?"

Sam shrugged, "Dean taught me."

"Dean doesn't seem the type to wear a tie, either."

"He's not, but he said 'it'll come in handy'. And that 'a real man knows many things, even if he doesn't always need them'."

"So, I'm not a real man then?"

"Not until tonight," Sam winked with a laugh.

"S-Sam! You just made your first dirty joke!" Gabriel wrapped him up in a hug. "I'm so proud of you!"

"Yeah-yeah it's sooo exciting."

"But it is! Oh, Sammich, you don't know how much this *means* to me. After all this time, so many *years*, I've finally *taught* you something!" Gabriel gushed and squeezed the giant tighter.

"Okay-okay you taught me something. Now get off me!"

*****

"There. Better?" Cas took a step back to examine his handiwork.

Gabriel ran an appreciative hand down the tie, "How does everyone else know how to do this but me?" He turned left and right to check himself from all angles in the mirror.

"You must've missed the meeting. There was a bulletin about it and everything," Cas smoothed Gabriel's shirt collar down over the tie around his neck.

"They should really send e-mails out, I'm telling you!" Gabriel flicked lint off his blazer and tugged on the lapels a bit to settle it against his shoulders more securely.

Cas took an appreciative step back, "You look good enough to be seen in public with *me*."

"Oh, puh-leeze…" Gabriel smirked. "You *wish* you looked this good. Hell, *everyone* wishes they looked this good. Okay," he clapped both his hands together in expectation, "let's light this candle. Before something happens."

Cas rolled his eyes. "Keep the pony in the corral, Mary. Now," he turned on his heel, "if you have no more *emergencies*, I'll get back to running the wedding. *Apparently* everyone else was dropped on their head as a child and is incapable of making a decision without me."

"If I look this good," Gabriel ignored his brother, "then Sam… Oh!" He put his hand over his heart, "Be still my heart. That gorgeous hunk of burning love…" He turned himself left and right again to make another examination of his outfit. Cocking his head to one side, he got a better view of how perky his ass looked in his suit pants and then checked-out his reflection head-on. He put his hands on his hips, "I wonder if Rough Rider makes flame-retardant condoms?"

*****

"You rang?" Dean asked with a smile as he let himself through the hotel suite door.

He looked around with a frown--there were clothes thrown all over the place, and Sam was in the closet throwing more out onto the ground. And he was still in a tank and boxers.

"What the hell, man. You're not dressed yet? We're supposed to start in a half-hour."

"Dean! My life's over. It's not here!" Sam gestured to the clothes on the ground, his eyes wild.

"…What's not here?"

"My tux! You know, the one Gabriel had *made* for me. For our *wedding*," Sam raked his fingers through his hair in agitation. "I know I packed it into the truck we sent ahead. It was in the black suit bag. It had a giant label that I wrote 'Sam's tux - do not touch' on with a Sharpie just to make sure we could find it. But it's not here!" Sam spun back around to throw more clothes on the ground.

"I'm sure it's here somewhere. We just gotta look for it. Okay?" Dean put his hands on his brother's shoulders in reassurance. "Just calm down. I'll help. I mean, how far could it go. Not like it grew legs, right?"

"Gabriel was so sweet. He booked me time in the spa. You should really go down there, by the way." He stopped whining momentarily to give his brother an aside about the spa, "I had one of those Rosemary Mint Awakening Body Wraps, y'know? I never knew peppermint could be used like that. Go ahead feel my skin. Seriously, touch it," he shoved his arm in front of Dean's face. "By the time I was done the ninety-minute Thai Massage, I was so relaxed. All I wanted to do was get dressed. And now I can't find my tux," Sam fanned himself. "This can't be happening. How could this have happened? I can't get married in my underwear!" Sam wailed, collapsing in a heap on the ground, holding his head in his hands.

"Whoa, hey… Relax, little brother. Don't go all drama queen on me now," Dean held his arms out in front of himself and made a calming gesture in Sam's direction.. "Look, just stay there. Don't worry about a thing. I'm the best man. I'm the guy who has your back. I'll go look for it, okay? I'll ask Cas. Cas will know. He knows *everything*," Dean assured him on his way out of the room

"I don't know…" Sam looked up with tears in his eyes, "Dean, what if he lost it?"

"You're kidding, right? This is Cas we're talking about. There's *no way* Cas lost your tux. He loves that thing possibly even more than you do. Seriously, we'll find it." Dean assured him before disappearing out the door in a hurry.

I hope.

*****

"Cas!" Dean yelled for his boyfriend. He caught sight of him disappearing into the reception hall. "*Marco!*"

"Polo-o-o!" Cas sang out and stuck his pen in the air to signal his location. "Can it wait? Kinda busy, hon," Cas barely looked up from his clipboard as he strode into the room.

"It really can't," Dean ran up to him and pecked him on the cheek. "We have a problem." He put a hand on his arm to get his attention. "Listen, Sam can't find his tux," he told him in a lowered tone.

"You shut your *mouth*," Cas's jaw bulged as he clenched his teeth and stopped dead in his tracks. He skewered him with a withering look, "That's not funny, babe."

"Well, I was just in his room. He tore the place apart. Aaand it's not there."

"No-no, that's impossible. I had it sent up to his room personally. It *has* to be in there. I already checked it off the to-do list." Cas flipped back a few pages on his clipboard and tapped at a line with the tip of his pen.

"I don't know what to tell you, man, but it's not there." Dean shrugged.

"No, see? It's the very first thing I did when we arrived. 'Item 1: Deliver Sam's tux to his room, Room 230,'" Cas read, tipping the clipboard to show the taller man.

"Please, don't take my head off, but… are you sure?" Not prone to drama, even Dean was starting to panic. He didn't want to see the day ruined for his little brother.

"You dare question me? Oh, honey. I had it delivered to room two-thirty, Morning Star, as soon as I got here," Cas mumbled, looking back over his notes.

"Wait, two-thirty? No, that's not right. Sam's not in room two-thirty."

"He is. And *Gabriel's* in room two-thirty. But in the other wing. I know because I'm the one who booked the rooms. There's two wings, Horizon and Morning Star, and the room numbers are the same," he held up a hand before Dean could say something. "Don't even. I *know*. I already had this conversation with the desk clerk," he rolled his eyes. "Gabriel needed a room on the west side, because none of the east side rooms have enough windows. They were further apart, but at least I didn't have to deal with Gabriel having a claustrophobic panic attack. I have enough to worry about, y'know."

Dean threw his hands in the air and pulled a face, "Well, whatever, okay? It's on the list, but I just came from Sam's room and I'm telling you, it's not there. He's still standing around in his underwear." Dean crossed his arms. "Ideas?"

Cas closed his eyes and rubbed at his temples with the tips of his fingers, "I smell burnt toast. Does anyone else smell that?" Cas dropped his hands from his temples, "The delivery driver had one job. *One job.* Did they not give him a map of this establishment? What did I pay him for? Let that be a lesson to you. Never tip until *after* you see the goods."

"Cas, focus. You said their room numbers are the same, right? Maybe it's not lost. What if... What if the courier just got the wings wrong and it's just in Gabriel's room?" Dean said with hope.

"No, I don't think so," Cas grumbled.

"Don't be so negative. Why?"

"Because I only saw one tux in Gabriel's room and he was wearing it."

"So, you think he's wearing Sam's tux? Seriously. And you wouldn't have noticed this? Remind me to take you to the eye doctor." Dean gave him a wink, "Sam's must be there."

"You think?"

"Yeah, I'm sure it was just an honest mistake with the wings and everything. I'll go check it out and we'll get it all sorted out and everything will be fine."

"Honest mistake, my sweet ass," Cas grumbled

Dean took him by the shoulders and leaned in close to his ear, "And speaking of your sweet ass, will I get to see that later?"

"*Dean*, focus," he pushed him off him with a smile. "You, go. I have a million and one things to do in the next," Cas pulled out his iPhone and check his itinerary, "twenty-four minutes *and counting*."

Dean grimaced, "I don't suppose there's a way to delay this a bit?"

Cas gave him the Look-Of-Death.

"Ooo-kay then. I'll just run back up, grab the tux from Gabriel's room, get Sam into it and we're golden," he clapped his hands together.

"Move it, Mister," he pointed him toward the door. "We're burning daylight!"

"Next time, I get to plan and you get to run around looking for your little brother."

Cas looked down his nose at him in judgement, "Honey, I love you, but you couldn't plan a peanut butter sandwich without me."

Dean was already heading out of the reception hall and called over his shoulder, "The *one time* I forgot to pick up peanut butter... You're never gonna let that one go."

"Hurry!"

"Don't tell me what to do!"

"I'm the *wedding planner*!" Cas hurled at his retreating back.

Damn it!

*****

"Gabriel, you decent?" Dean called, knocking on the door.

"Gabriel?" He called again after a moment of silence.

He opened the door and stuck his head in, scanning the room for the trouble-maker, but not finding him. A man on a mission, he let himself in and hurried to the closet to look for Sam's suit. "Gabriel?" He called over his shoulder while he dug around, "Dude, quit playing around."

After not finding the suit with Gabriel's other clothes, he took a tour of the room. It wasn't that big, there were only so many places the suit could be. When it became clear it wasn't there, he stopped in the centre of the room with his hands on his hips. Now he had two problems. The groom was missing. "Fuck," he hung his head in defeat. "Cas is gonna kill me."

He pulled out his phone with a heavy sigh, "How's my favourite wedding planner?"

"*What?*"

"We have another problem."

"*No.*"

"Cas…"

"Fine. What is it *now.*"

"Uh, I can't find Gabriel."

*****

Okay-okay. It'll be fine. Dean'll come in any minute holding the tux and it'll be okay. I can get married. Nothing's ruined. My life isn't over... Sam prowled around his room, working to keep himself from going Total Drama Queen as his brother would say.

He plopped himself down on the bed, *Oh, who am I kidding? I wrecked the wedding! How the hell could I lose it? I'm so stupid... Everybody came all the way over here and got all dressed-up for nothing and now I'm going to have to go out there and explain how we need to postpone the damn thing all because-*

Music from outside broke through his thoughts. He frowned and got up to investigate. Opening the window, he peered down to the source of the music.

His soon-to-be-husband was standing on the lawn under his window holding an old school boom box over his head. "Gabriel?"

"Hey, Sammich," the hazel-eyed man gave him a huge grin.

"What're you doing?" He laughed despite himself. "You're crazy."

"*I wish I could carry, your smile in my heart.*" Gabriel sang up to the second floor, adorably off-key.

Sam chuckled and shook his head--even at his own wedding Gabriel was causing trouble.

"How did you find a radio station that plays this?"

"Let's just say I made a special request," Gabriel replied with a wink, lowering the volume. "Would you care to join me?" He raised an eyebrow in mischief and nodded in the direction of the gardens.

"What? We can't *leave*. Get up here," he couldn't help but laugh while Gabriel continued to make silly running away motions with his fingers. "We're getting *married!*"

"Gumdrop, it's *our* wedding. They can't exactly start it without us."

"But... I'm kind of in the middle of looking for something." Sam looked back at the mess in his room.

"Oh, c'mon! How can you resist me when I look this good? I mean, look at me! Whatever it is it can wait."

"*Gabriel...*"

"Come down from your tower my prince! Or shall I come up?" He asked with an over-exaggerated wink. "I'll just shimmy up this drainpipe here and-"

"No! Oh, my God, you *are* crazy," he couldn't help but laugh. "No-no. I'll come down."

"Yay!"

How am I supposed to get down? Sam examined the outside of the building.

"Jump," Gabriel suggested, putting the stereo down beside him and holding his arms out.

"Um, no, I'm not gonna *jump.*"

"Sammy c'mon! It's either that or *you* climb down that drainpipe." Gabriel nodded toward it.

"I'll take my chances with the pipe." Sam replied with a smile.

Gabriel watched Sam get himself onto the window ledge and then grab for the pipe.

"I can't reach it!" Sam exclaimed, looking down, half-relieved.

"Reach you giant freak!" Gabriel goaded, turning the stereo off.

Sam stretched himself out farther, barely grasping the pipe in his one hand. He took a deep breath and jumped at it, grabbing it with his other hand without falling. Gabriel wolf whistled at the view of the brunette's ass hanging over his head and watched with half-amusement, half-arousal as it shimmied down the pipe.

"What I wouldn't give to be that pipe right now…"

"Shut up," he threw down at his fiancée in amusement.

Sam landed on the ground with a soft *thud* and straightened his tank top and shorts as Gabriel came to meet him.

"That wasn't so hard, was it?" Gabriel pulled Sam in for a kiss.

Sam nuzzled his neck, "Isn't it bad luck for us to see each other before the wedding?"

"Well, by the looks of things," Gabriel looked up and down at Sam's not-so-dressed self, "there isn't anything *here*," he hooked a finger into the waistband of Sam's boxers and tugged on the fabric to take a peek, "I haven't seen before. Besides, if it *was* bad luck, you probably would've died climbing down that thing."

"Oh, gee, thanks."

"Shall we?" Gabriel offered his elbow.

Sam slipped his hand through the loop of his lover's arm, "What are you planning?"

"It wouldn't be a surprise if you knew, now, would it?"

Sam sighed and snuggled closer. Why fight it? He knew from experience it was best to just go along for the ride. Questions would get him nowhere. They walked along for a while in silence, enjoying the scenery as they passed the fountain at the front of the property. Gabriel walked them over to the gardens, but instead of heading for the entrance, made a sharp turn right into the hedge fence around the edge of the property, giving Sam a face full branches.

"Sorry," he pulled him along with him as he pushed branches out of their way.

Sam swatted at more branches, "Where are we going, Narnia?"

"That would be in the back of a wardrobe," Gabriel corrected with a small smile.

"Fine," Sam grumbled. "Then what the hell's behind a giant hedge?"

"*This*," Gabriel gestured, as they finally broke through and out the other side.

A large green pasture spread out before them, enclosed on two sides by hedges and a small pond on the right.

"Gabriel, this… It's beautiful," Sam stammered, breathless.

"I know, right?" The shorter man glowed.

He took an awe-struck Sam's hand and led him closer to the water. A smile lit up his features as he heard Sam caught his breath and let himself be led to what he'd describe as a 'picture perfect' picnic. There were all of his favourite foods on top of the old blanket they'd owned back when they first moved in together.

"H-how did- I thought you threw this out ages ago?" Sam dropped to his knees and reached out to feel it.

"You told me to get rid of it, but I just... couldn't. I guess you could say I thought I might need it someday," Gabriel took a seat beside him.

"How... Back then, you already knew?" Sam looked up at his face.

"I didn't. I just... hoped," Gabriel shrugged with a lop-sided grin.

Stunned, Sam looked back at the picnic in front of him-- half the food there he swore he only mentioned once in front of him. Some he was sure he'd never actually mentioned out loud. *Where did he get these? I haven't seen those since I was a kid,* and it was all cut up into cute, bite-sized heart shapes.

"I think this is the mushiest thing you've ever done for me," Sam looked into his eyes with a smile.

"Wait until you hear my vows."

*****

"What do you mean you lost *both* of them?" Cas was ready to kill someone.

"*I* didn't lose them. They're not in their rooms!" Dean worked hard to defend himself, but it wasn't doing much good. He crossed his arms in frustration.

"Then where the hell did they *go?*"

"I don't know. But they're nowhere. No one's seen them."

"The wedding is in, what, fifteen minutes and we're *missing both grooms!*" Cas was verging on an aneurism and looked like he was about to pass out.

"Whoa, hey, babe. Take a breath. We'll find them, okay?" Dean slung an arm around his boyfriend to make sure he didn't fall over. "Don't worry. Maybe they just went to the bathroom?"

Cas gave him a withering look, "At the same time?"

"Hey, man, we *are* talking about Gabriel here. They're probably... y'know..." He shrugged, helpless, "Practicing for the honeymoon and lost track of time," he finished with a weak laugh.

"Not helping."

"Well, hey, Sam couldn't have gone far, because we didn't find the tux yet, so-" Dean bit his tongue, instantly regretting the words when he saw the colour drain from Cas' face.

Cas's voice went up another octave, "You mean you didn't *find the tux yet?*"

"It wasn't in Gabriel's room and he wasn't there when I got there, either. I figured they were together, so I went back to Sammy's room, but when I got back there *he* wasn't in *his* room."

"Oh-God-oh-God-oh-God..." Cas looked green. "This is a disaster."

"Don't worry, I'll figure something out," Dean worked to stay positive.

"What are *you* going to do?" Cas regarded him with hopeless eyes, "What are *we* going to do?"

"Tell you what, you make sure everything else is ready, and I'll go get them and make sure they're both runway ready." Dean patted him on the shoulder and pushed him on his way.

"How are you going to do that in *fifteen minutes*? You don't even know where they *are.*"

"Babe," Dean gave him a wink before running off, "It's what I do."

*****

"Don't we need to be getting back?" Sam asked as they strolled along the water's edge, interlacing their fingers.

"Naw, like I said before, honey. It's *our* wedding."

"Won't they be worried?"

Gabriel raised an eyebrow, "Do you really want to go back to all that running around crap?"

"No… I just feel bad. I mean, what if they're looking for us?"

Gabriel chucked quietly, "I have no doubt they are. But what does it matter? This is about us. And the wedding starts whenever we show up."

"Cas is going to kill you, y'know," now Sam was chuckling. "You'll be lucky if you make it to the reception once he gets his hands on you."

"Let me handle my brother." Gabriel stopped them walking, so he could face his soon-to-be-husband. "Sammy," he took his other hand, "what are you really worried about?"

"I just… my suit's missing- That's why I'm not dressed." He avoided his eyes.

"Sammy, *that's* why you're so worried?"

"Yeah. I can't marry you in my boxers! I just wanted to look good and now the suit's missing. The one you had made for me," Sam pouted. "I have no idea where it went."

"Sam, you always look great," Gabriel pecked the back of his hand.

"I just wanted to look special for you," he frowned.

Gabriel sighed and shook his head. He took in the sad puppy face in front of him and melted. "All right," he said with a sigh of indulgent resignation, "guess I better give you your other surprise then." Gabriel let go of Sam's hands and strode away from him.

"What other surprise?" Sam asked after him, but Gabriel didn't answer. "What other surprise?"

Gabriel led them over to the other side of the pasture where the hedges were and tried to hold in his smile as they reached the suit bag he'd hung there earlier that day.

"Gabriel, what is this?"

"Well, there was some sort of mix-up and *this*," he gestured to himself, "was supposed to be your suit. But I figured you'd want to wear this instead."

Giving him a questioning, but excited look, Sam pulled the zipper down the length of the bag. Holding his breath, he pushed the covering back behind the hanger to reveal a custom-tailored, pitch-black suit. And a very expensive one from the look of it.

"Gabriel…" Sam breathed.

"Wait. Look in the pocket," Gabriel nodded toward the jacket, unable to contain his smile any longer.

Curious as to what else he could have possibly done, Sam reached into the breast pocket of the jacket and pulled out a handkerchief, the corners folded, so the name 'Samilicious' sparkled up at him.

"I know it doesn't look like much, but I did the emerald studding myself." Gabriel said from behind him in a low voice.

"My birthstone?" Sam inspected the lettering in amazement. "Honey, it's beautiful."

"Yeah?" Gabriel asked, relaxing a little.

"I love it," Sam looked up from the gift to wrap him up in a hug.

"Good." Gabriel nuzzled his neck, "But there's still more."

"What else could you-"

"Don't question. Just unwrap," Gabriel let him go and stepped back.

With care, Sam unwrapped the handkerchief, no idea what more there could be. He unveiled a worn and folded piece of paper. Sam flicked his eyes up to his lover and at his nod, he carefully unfolded the paper. Once he got it unfolded, he saw every line on the page completely filled with Gabriel's handwriting.

"What is this?" Sam took his time, absorbing one line after another, his smile widening with each line.

"It's a, uh, list," Gabriel's face grew red.

"Yeah, I can see that, silly. What's it a list *of*?" Sam's eyes flicked up to look at him.

"It's a thousand promises. For a thousand ways to show you I love you."

In that moment, he wished he had a camera, because the look of love and amazement on Sam's face was definitely worth remembering. He would never forget it, but he wished he could preserve it in an album. It would stay in his heart forever and no matter how many other moments they might have between them, this would always be his number one. He had lied to him about one thing, though--when he said he had only hoped they'd end up together when they first moved in. That was a lie. He knew after the first time he set eyes on him. There was never any doubt. Back when they were six, he knew he had to make him his.

"*You two, freeze!*" Dean's strident voice shattered the moment. "*You are in so much trouble!*"

"Dean. Uh, how did you find us?" Sam folded the paper up and put it back in the suit pocket, so it would sit over his heart while he was making his vows.

"Well it wasn't easy, that's for sure. Do you know what time it is? What the hell are you doing out here? Do you know you almost gave Cas a heart attack? What is wrong with you, disappearing fifteen minutes before you're supposed to get married?" Dean ranted, looking back and forth between them. He gestured angrily at Sam, "And you're *still* not dressed yet?"

"Whoa, hey, calm down Dean-o. Last I checked it was *our* wedding." Gabriel cocked an impish eyebrow at the blonde, "I thought that meant it couldn't start without us?"

"Well, okay then, would *you* like to be the one to tell Cas that?" Dean countered, with a pointed look.

"Okay-okay," Gabriel laughed. "No need to panic. We'll be right there."

Dean squinted accusatorily at him, but stomped off a few feet, whipping out his cell phone.

Gabriel turned back to Sam, looking expectant, "Guess we better go get married now, huh?" He kicked at the dirt like a love struck teenager.

"I think that'd be a good idea," Sam chuckled, pulling him in for a kiss.

"I love you Sammich."

"I love you, too."

"Let's *go,* people!" Dean yelled to them, tapping his watch dramatically. "We're already two hours late and Cas is going to have your organs on a spit."

"Okay-okay! Jesus, he's pushy," Gabriel snagged the suit off the bush and took Sam's hand.

"That he is," Sam agreed with a chuckle.

"You ready?"

"Well, I'll probably need to put the suit *on,*" Sam replied with a chuckle.

"Yeah, I don't think Cas would be impressed if you walked down the aisle in your underwear," Gabriel smirked.

"Exactly. Even though I know *you* wouldn't mind."

"I'm going to rip you out of it as soon as I get the chance. It's a waste of a suit, really," Gabriel said with fake disappointment.

"Look on the bright side."

"That we're getting married?"

"Nope. That you'll get the rest of your life to rip me out of my clothes."

"Oh Sammy, you're still so naïve," Gabriel sighed, kissing his hand.

"What?"

"You really think I'd let you continue wearing clothes?"

Your Heart's A Liar!

"I love you."

The whisper was both the best and worst thing he'd ever heard come from those lips.

"I-I love you, too," Sam's voice shook as he tried to hold back fresh tears.

"I need to go now."

The statement shattered the man's heart, still wishing he didn't have to go and that they could go on pretending for just a little while longer.

"I'll come back."

The promise broke him apart wider and he closed his eyes as his tears betrayed him, "I know."

*****

"Sammy?"

The voice made Sam blink, but otherwise he didn't move. Dean took the silence as an invitation. He opened the bedroom door and came in.

"Jesus! Would it kill you to turn on a light?" He asked with a laugh, walking cautiously into the room.

Dean had never seen his brother this wrecked. All he did was sit in the old wooden chair they'd found him in, starring at the wall. Dean had wanted to burn that damn chair the second they arrested that psycho, but Sam had been adamant about keeping it. In fact, that was the last time he remembered Sam speaking. The doctors said it was just PTSD and that it would pass as long as he gave Sam space to deal with it. Dean wasn't convinced. He knew there was more. Seeing his brother like this--a shell of who he once was-- seemed more like he was going through withdrawal or a bad break-up instead of recovering from being kidnapped.

Hell, he never talked anymore and only showered when Dean managed to pull him out of the chair. There was no way he could leave him to fend for himself, so right after it happened, Dean had moved in to look after him. Though time had passed, Sam refused to move or come down for meals forcing Dean to bring them up on a tray. Even then, he still barely ate what his brother brought him. It had been three days since the last time Dean saw any of the food touched, *All two bites of the sandwich.* He was getting way too thin for Dean's liking. This couldn't go on for much longer.

"You hungry, Sammy?" Dean asked cheerfully, placing the tray of food down on the bed.

At least, he stopped cringing at the nickname. That's an improvement, Dean didn't even want to *think* about what his brother endured. Just knowing what he'd done to the previous victims was bad enough, but imagining that being done to his *brother*... Whatever that guy had done, he made Sam scared of his own nickname. When they burst in and found him, Dean had called out for him and he wigged-out, crying hysterically and jumped back a mile.

Dean walked over to the curtained window that was on the wall Sam faced and tore the drapes open, sunlight flooding the room. Even this only got the giant to lower his head, hair falling over his face, instead of the usual sharp cry and jerk of his head to escape it. Dean didn't always open the drapes, but it couldn't be doing him any good sitting in the dark day after day. At first, he couldn't seem to stand the light at all, and his reaction was more vocal and violent. Now, he didn't seem to have that kind of energy, but he still didn't like it. Sam hissed at him as he jerked his head away.

Still no words, Not surprised, but still mildly disappointed.

"C'mon Sammy. It's good for you," Dean sighed. After a moment's consideration, he went over to get a better look at his brother.

Sam didn't look up. Dean grabbed him by the chin and forced his face up. Tear tracks ran down his cheeks below his eyes, turned red and puffy by weeks of silent weeping. The lines of stress and sadness now seemed permanently etched into the youngers' face. It was sad. He'd aged. He'd been young before the kidnapping, but now his face showed a lifetime of pain.

Those are fresh tear stains…

"You been crying again?" Dean was surprised. *How long is this going to go on? I thought he was passed this now.*

Sam wrenched his chin out from his brother's hand and dropped his head, hair falling to hide his features again.

"He can't hurt you anymore, Sammy," Dean's voice was soft and earnest. "I promise. You don't need to worry. You're safe now." Dean continued to watch him for a few moments, but he didn't react. With reluctance, he turned back to the door.

He paused in the doorway, taking one more look at his brother, *God, I hate that it looks like you can't get away. You can. You can walk out of this room anytime. You just have to want to.*

His heart heavy, Dean closed the door softly behind him, *I miss you Sammy.*

*****

Not two minutes after Dean left, Sam jumped out of his chair and closed the curtains. The light hurt his eyes too much for him to see.

"How many times have I told you the light hurts my eyes!" Sam yelled, voice hoarse from lack of use, smacking his hands against the wall in anger. "But don't worry Dean, I fixed it!"

"Sam…" He heard the voice and froze.

"Y-you can't be here," the giant stuttered, going back to his chair.

"Why not?" The voice asked and he could hear the smirk.

"They took you away." Sam mumbled, closing his eyes and picturing his outline in the dark, tears pricking at his eyes.

"They could never keep me away from you, Sam."

He swore he could feel the warm breath against his ear.

"How long?" Sam asked, voice shaking.

"As soon as I get out, I'm coming straight to you."

*****

"You know I'd never hurt you right, Sammy?"

Luce was staring at him across the breakfast table, his face blank. *Oh man, he's doing it again,* Sam examined his expression closely. *Why does he always choose to do this over breakfast?* Sam took a sip of his coffee, "I know," he said after a long beat. He watched him absorb the answer, waiting for a reaction. This seemed to satisfy the blonde, because without saying another word, he nodded to himself and went back to his food. His face grew animate again and it was as if he'd never said a word.

Sam watched him in silence for another moment. "You okay?" Sam asked with concern.

Luce shoved the last bite of toast into his mouth, "Uh, yeah," he laughed. "Are *you* okay?" In sudden good spirits, he jumped up and put his dishes in the sink. "I hate to eat and run, but I gotta go to work, Blossom."

"Blossom?" Sam laughed despite himself, his tension breaking, "That's a new one."

Luce raised an eyebrow, "What? I'm trying it out." He squinted, "No good?"

"Works better than Sugar Lips, but still a 'no'."

"Damn," Luce grabbed his jacket. "But if I remember correctly, you seemed to *love* Sugar Lips. I thought your hysterical laughing was a good thing."

Sam stood from the table, "Have a good day," the sentiment dripped sarcasm.

Luce snorted

"C'mon. Try not to let the customers get the better of you."

"It's not *my* fault they're stupid," Luce grumbled.

"Fine. Then just promise me you won't *tell* any of them this time," Sam chuckled, wrapping his arms around his partner.

"Fine," he sighed dramatically.

"If you're good, you might even get a little surprise when you get back," Sam gave him a wink.

"Oh yeah?"

"Yep. But only if you behave."

"Yes, Sir!" Luce snapped off a salute.

Sam chuckled at his sudden enthusiasm and pressed a kiss to his lips, revelling in the way they felt.

"I looove youuu," Luce sang, pressing his body closer to his lover.

"I know," Sam chuckled. "Now go to work." Letting go, he sat back down to his breakfast.

"All right, I'll be back around seven." Luce gave him another quick kiss before running out the kitchen door.

"Sam?" He heard his brother call from the front door.

"Back here!" Sam called back, getting up to meet him in the front hallway.

"Luce?" Dean asked, looking around with suspicion.

"You just missed him."

"Good."

"*Dean*," Sam groaned.

"I don't trust him. I can't help it."

Sam rolled his eyes, "You've never even *met* him."

"Exactly. Don't you think it's a little suspicious that you've been with him for four months and every time I come over I 'just miss' him?"

"No, you just suck at timing." Sam stuck his tongue out before turning back to the kitchen.

"Or he's avoiding me," Dean followed behind him.

"Why would he be avoiding you? He doesn't even know you."

"I don't know. Maybe he's hiding something he doesn't want your detective brother to find out."

"Don't you have a robber to catch or something?" Rather than sit at the table, Sam leaned himself against the counter to face his brother.

"Kidnapper, actually," Dean stole a piece of toast off Sam's plate. "And I still got time before I need to leave."

"How's the search going?" Sam tried diverting the conversation.

"Don't change the subject," Dean took a bite of toast.

"I wasn't."

"Did," Dean sat at the table.

"You're the laziest detective I know," Sam muttered.

"I'm the *only* detective you know," Dean countered with an angelic smile.

"Well if they're all like you, one's more than enough," Sam rolled his eyes.

Dean opened his mouth to show him the chewed-up toast in response.

"Ew, dude. You're disgusting!"

The green-eyed man just shrugged and closed his mouth, swallowing before taking a sip from Sam's coffee.

"Oookay, that's enough free food for you." Sam stalked to the door and held it open, looking pointedly at his brother.

"All right, all right. I can take a hint." Dean wiped his hands on his pants before standing up.

"Good." Sam pointed out the open door, "Get out."

"I'm just looking out for you, Sammy."

"Goodbye, Dean." Sam replied sarcastically. *I'll be fine.*

*****

"Look Doc, I'm telling you, he's getting worse!" Dean paced across the living room floor in agitation. After his examination of his brother that morning, in growing concern, he had called the doctor and convinced him to make yet another house call. But he couldn't seem to make him understand.

"I appreciate your concern, Detective, but I can assure you, it's all part of the healing process. This isn't that unusual," the doctor's tone was meant to be reassuring.

"He's still not eating," Dean turned on his heal to go back the other way.

"Your brother is fine. You need to let him heal at his own pace."

"But-"

"No *buts.* He's healing. He just needs more time. You know the expression *'things get worse before they get better'*?"

"Yeah, but-"

"The same is true for people. During recovery, sometimes a patient will appear to be growing worse, but they're really getting better. It's quite understandable. There's a lot of internal healing that needs to take place here, as well, remember. Especially for as severe a case of PTSD as this was. This is as well as we can expect right now. The best thing you can do for him is continue to give him the support he needs." The doctor picked up his medical bag, bringing the conversation to a close.

"Is there anything else I can do for him? To help him get over this faster?" Dean ran a worried hand through his hair. This was no good, "You're giving me nothing here, y'know." And he couldn't continue to do nothing. Prone to action, he wanted him better. Now. He hated that so much of this was outside his control.

"You're doing more than enough to help. He'll be all right, Detective." Despite his impatience, he strove to be reassuring, "Trust me."

"Please, I'm begging you here. Can't you just take a look at him again?" Dean stopped pacing and pinned him with a pleading look.

"I'm sorry, but there's nothing else I can do here." The doctor's patience was beginning to wear thin, "As hard as I know this is for you, you need to back off. He really just needs time to himself."

"That's the only thing he has right now," Dean mumbled, crossing his arms. "And that doesn't make it okay."

"I'm sorry Detective, I hate to be rude, but I have another appointment." The doctor side-stepped around Dean and strode to the door, "I'll see myself out."

"No, hang on," Dean gave him a soulful look and followed him to the front hall. "I appreciate you coming out," Dean leaned against the doorframe. "This is just tough for me, y'know. I hate seeing him like this."

"I know it's hard. But hang in there," the doctor clapped him on the shoulder. "Be strong for him, that's what he needs right now. That's all," The doctor slipped out the door, "Call me if there's any major change," he said over his shoulder as he headed to his car.

Fuck! Dean slammed the door shut and kicked a chair over on his way back to the living room, running his hands through his hair in distraction. "All right. Okay," he breathed deeply, closing his eyes while he worked to quell the rage, so he could think straight. "You won't help me? Fine. I'll find someone who will."

*****

"Are you *sure* this intel's correct?" Surprised, Dean skimmed the file in his hand again. His team had been working on this kidnapping case for ages. This was one of the biggest cases of his career, probably *the* biggest. When they caught that bastard, they'd probably pin a medal on his chest and give him a promotion.

"Yes, Sir. I double checked it myself." Frank, his Detective Corporal and right hand man, confirmed. Frank eyed his team leader with nervousness. He knew how important this case was for all of them. "What do you think?"

This was just the break they needed. He narrowed his eyes in concentration, "Based on the pattern we established, do we know when he's taking his next victim?" Dean flipped the file closed and tossed it onto his desk.

"All signs point to tonight. Before he makes a run for the border. He knows we're on to him now. No way he's sticking around. But he'll do it again before he goes. He's predictable."

"Yeah. Almost too predictable," he said to himself. He glanced back at the file and then back at Frank, "Looks like this is our shot then," he nodded. "Okay, get the team together and we'll get everyone up to speed. Let's be ready to go for seven." Dean pulled his shoulder holster out of his top desk drawer and threw it across his back.

"You got it, Serg," Frank scurried off to round up the troops.

Dean ran his eyes over the whiteboard. Every piece of info they'd gathered about the kidnapper taunted him--the multiple victims' faces told the tale of their defeat to this point. *It's your fault we're dead.* The Feds had their jurisdiction over serial killers and were working their own theories, but while they might have compelled him to relinquish his lead on it, he couldn't let it go.

He knew he could get him.

The evidence built the story of the monster behind the murders. At first, there was nothing, but with each victim, he had grown more bold. After a while, patterns began to emerge and now lay out before him like a map. Over that time, it also appeared he was getting sloppy, but Dean knew that wasn't the case. The newspapers might have had their pet names for him, but Dean just thought of him as the Monster. And the Monster was taunting him--what appeared to be mistakes he knew were careful clues toward a purpose. He just didn't know what that was yet. *But I will soon.*

As long as the Feds stayed out of his way.

He always felt a sense of excitement before a take-down--from his first 'matching the description' call as a rookie he was hooked. He loved the thrill of the chase, the rush. Craved it, even as his heightened sense of justice made it so much more. Maybe even something righteous. Righteous protection of the weak. It was that thing that beat in every good cop's chest, but that they never spoke about, because it was too corny for a bunch of hardasses to admit to each other. But it was true. Always a sucker for a good take-down, it would be a righteous bust that would protect so many others and he was proud to do it. The guy was taunting him, inviting him even, *it would be my pleasure.* He looked over the board again containing the kidnapper's essence and smiled.

"No more games. Tonight? You're mine."

*****

"Sammy! I'm home!" Luce called, coming in the front door.

"Hey! How was work?" Sam greeted him with a kiss.

"I was *very* good today," he grabbed the giant's hips and pulled him against his own body.

"Oh, really now?" Sam ran a hand up through Luce's hair, smirking. He loved seeing him like this, playful and affectionate. It was going to be a great night. Sam relaxed against him.

"Yes, Sir. Didn't even tell the customer who asked me where we 'sold the Internet' that they were too stupid to buy it," Luce boasted.

"Wow, that must have taken some restraint," Sam chuckled.

"You have *no* idea," Luce kissed him on the tip of the nose. "So... Do I get my surprise?" Luce's eyes lit up with excitement.

"Surprise? I don't know..." Sam pretended to think about it.

"Awww, but I was so good. Just like I promised." Luce whined and pecked him on the cheek, "C'mon, I earned it, right?" He pecked him on the other cheek. And then covered his whole face in kisses until he gave in.

"All right, all right. You'll get your surprise."

"Great," Luce attacked Sam's neck.

"Whoa! N-not yet. We gotta eat first," Sam backed out of his arms and lead him into the kitchen.

"Awww."

"Hey, I worked hard, too. All for you."

"I'm sorry. It smells delicious," Luce stepped up to one of the pots.

"Hey!" Sam swatted his hand away, "Wash your hands before you stick them in there."

"Oh, c'mon, just a little-"

"*No*. Wash," Sam directed him to the sink.

"Fine," Luce grumbled and sighed dramatically. At the sink, he made a large production out of washing his hands.

"Good boy," Sam chuckled, stirring the sauce.

"Okay, I'm washed," Luce held up his clean hands in evidence. "I can taste it now, right?" He dried his hands on his shirt.

"Yes, *now* you can try it." Sam put the spoon down and stepped out of the way.

"Good," Luce breathed, coming up behind him, he sucked on his neck.

"Mmm… I-I thought you wanted to taste dinner?" Sam grabbed the edge of the counter as his knees buckled in surprise.

"I am," Luce growled, sending a shiver through his lover.

Sam closed his eyes, turning his head more, so he could have better access.

"You just relax. Don't worry about a thing. Let me take care of you..," he purred.

Sam sighed in response and felt himself break out into goose bumps as he sucked lightly on his ear. Luce flipped him around roughly and attacked his lover's lips, making him lean back involuntarily against the counter to keep his balance. Luce sucked on his bottom lip a bit before gently turning his head to the side and kissed a trail down from his mouth to the other side of his neck.

Sam moaned, pressing himself tighter against the blonde in an effort to gain more friction.

"That's right, Sammy," Luce breathed, lightly blowing against his ear, earning him another shiver from the brunette.

"M-maybe we should move this upstairs," Sam suggested breathlessly.

"Exactly what I was thinking."

And then Sam felt a sharp pain in his neck.

He instinctively pushed Luce away from him and his hand went up to his neck in surprise.

"Did you just… bite me?" When he brought his hand away, he saw blood. But he was already dizzy and it was hard to think.

Luce just stood there, an unreadable look on his face. Sam's eyes drifted down to his hand and he saw the syringe.

"What the hell..?" He slurred in confusion, taking a staggering step forward.

Luce dropped the syringe and stepped closer, "Don't worry, I'll catch you."

"C-catch me…?" Sam trailed off as his body swayed forward.

Luce caught him before he face-planted into the table.

*****

"Wh…" Sam came-to slowly, blinking his blurry eyes to see, but there was nothing.

"It's okay, Sammy." Luce's gentle voice floated to him in the dark from somewhere off to his left. "The room's pitch black."

There was something oddly calming about the dark. Almost as if it were a safety blanket, protecting him from whatever was going to happen. "Where are we?" Sam strained his eyes in the dark, working to make out details while they adjusted.

"In the spare room."

"You drugged me." It was a statement. No question what Luce had done. What he didn't know was why.

"Only to make this easier."

"Make what easier?" Sam turned his head in the direction Luce's voice came from, "Are you okay?"

"Don't worry, my Blossom. I told you before. It's going to be okay."

Concerned, Sam moved to reach out a hand to find Luce in the dark. But realized his arms were bound. "You tied me up..?" Then he also tried to move his legs with no luck. "*Luce*, what the hell?"

"Temporarily."

"Oh, well that makes it better," Sam rolled his eyes, growing more concerned by the moment.

He felt Luce press his lips into the side of his neck, nuzzling him softly in comfort.

"Luce…" Sam relaxed without meaning to. But he didn't want to. He was really mad at Luce for all the mystery. He just wanted to snuggle in bed with him and have him try out more silly nicknames and go back to their first 'I love you' before Luce began acting strangely and when things were still simple. He didn't know what was going on, but he *did* know they weren't simple any more.

"Shhh," he cooed.

Maybe I can fix you..? "N-no. *Stop*," his voice hard. "Tell me what's going on."

He heard the blonde sigh and pull away. After a long moment he spoke, "I'm being sent to Illinois," his voice shook.

"And?" Sam prompted.

"I need to be there." He paused again. "A few months."

"Okay..? We already talked about that. We knew they'd send you eventually," Sam didn't see the problem.

He heard him sigh again and pictured him running his hands through his hair.

"Luce, I don't understand-"

"You can't come with me."

"...What?" Sam felt the breath get knocked out of him.

"I-I can't take you with me. I'm sorry." Luce drew closer to him again.

"Why not?" Tears prickled at his eyes, as he realized what he was saying.

"I just... I can't. It's not right," Luce explained without inflection.

"Wha-? Not right?" None of this made any sense. "What are you going to be doing?"

"I'm sorry, Sammy."

*****

"We set?" Dean looked around at the squad in front of him.

Everyone around the room nodded, their eyes hard and anxious, jacked-up and ready to come to the rescue of the first victim they had a chance to save.

"All right, Operation Bedtime's a go. Let's roll, people!" He commanded, leading the way out of the building and to the parking lot.

"What's the Sandman's location?" Dean hopped into the back of the lead van., tightening the Velcro of his Flak jacket.

"Lilac and Jordan Avenue." Frank spoke over his shoulder as he slid into the driver's seat.

"Lilac and Jordan Avenue?" Dean's heart rate increasing slightly. "Are you sure?"

"Yeah." Frank asked, looking at him in the rear view, "Problem?"

"No. No problem," Dean mumbled as they started the van.

Sammy...

*****

"I don't want to be without you," Luce rested his forehead against the brunette's.

"Then don't..."

Luce was sitting curled in his lap, crying softly, tears leaking onto Sam's cheeks. "It's not that easy."

"But why?" Sam couldn't hold back his own tears. This wasn't how it was supposed to go.

Luce didn't answer for a long moment, his tears taking his words. "I'm not who you think I am, Sam." Luce mumbled

"Who you think you are doesn't matter. Who I know you are does."

"Sammy..." Luce swallowed down the rest of the statement. "I can't let you know... what I've done..."

"Can't be worse than what you're doing now."

"I don't deserve you."

"You can't... you can't just *leave*," Sam sobbed, "not like this."

"I wish I could take you with me, believe me. But I don't want to drag you down with me," he pressed a kiss to his lips.

"What are you talking about?" Sam sniffed.

*****

"We sure he's in there?" Dean asked, swallowing thickly.

"Affirmative. Jose saw him go in there a couple minutes ago. There hasn't been any movement."

Dean nodded, but kept his eyes on the house, looking for any sign of activity. As soon as they had turned onto his brother's street, his heart refused to move out of his throat, but it wasn't until they stopped on the other side of the street and read out Sam's house number that it became apparent he forgot to put on deodorant that morning.

"Okay," he swallowed again, wiping his sweating palms on his pants, "we know he's in there. Are we clear to engage?"

"Still waiting on confirmation he's taken a hostage or if he's just setting up," Frank reported.

"Right. Let's get more eyes on this. We can't move until we get the whole picture. Frank, take a couple of the guys and stake-out that perimeter. Get me some better intel."

A knock on the van door made Dean jump and he opened it nervously, but relaxed as Jose hoped in.

"You okay, Boss? You don't look so good." He closed the door behind him.

"Yeah, I'm fine." Dean checked his gear again, "Jose, anything? We need to nab this monster before he slips past us and vanishes again. I'm not about to put another civilian in harm's way, but hostage or no hostage, we need to be all over this."

"The place is dark, Serg. We can't confirm what room he's in. I don't wanna go in blind. Just waiting on back-up now. Had to side-step the Feds, so they're delayed. Should be here in twenty." Frank gave Dean a concerned look.

"So, we just sit here?" Dean raised an eyebrow.

""Fraid so Boss." Jose furrowed his brow as he took in Dean's growing agitation, "Why you so antsy, man?"

Dean looked him in the eye, his voice dark, "That's my brother's house."

*****

"Sammy, my handsome Sammy. A thousand miles... I can't ... I can't have you a thousand miles away from me. How am I supposed to live with you a thousand miles away for so long?" Luce's voice was hollow as he sobbed harder into his shoulder.

"Why can't I just come with you? Please, Luce. I don't want to be without you," Sam begged, still not understanding why he couldn't go.

"Sammy..," he breathed, wrapping his arms around his neck.

"C-can't you quit?" Sam sniffed.

Luce barked out a bitter laugh and he felt him shake his head, "It's too late for that now." Sam closed his eyes, trying to soak up the warmth of his body against his own, taking the small comfort it provided. He wanted to hug him, but was stopped by the ropes. "Please, *please* let me hold you," he begged.

Luce sniffed and lifted his head, reaching behind his lover, undoing the ropes that held his arms against the chair, but left his wrists tied. Without hesitation, Sam brought his arms around in front of him, slipping them over the blonde's head to crush him to his chest. It was so good to feel him in his arms, warm and real against him.

"There you go... there you go..." Luce muttered against his chest, new tears pouring out of his eyes and soaking his shirt.

"H-how am I supposed to live without holding you in my arms?" Sam asked, squishing him impossibly harder into his chest, his own tears matting the blonde's hair.

*****

"That's my brother in there! We're going in five, whether you're here or not!" Dean flipped the burner phone closed before hurling it at the van wall.

"Tell the team to be ready to go on my mark," Dean ordered, turning to Jose. Fuck back-up, they were going in.

"But, Dean-"

"Understood?" He asked icily--all traces of rage gone.

"U-understood, Sir." Without further protest, Jose, grabbed his radio to relay the orders.

Hold on Sammy.

*****

"I love you."

The whisper was both the best and worst thing he'd ever heard come from those lips.

"I-I love you, too," Sam's voice shook as he tried to hold back fresh tears.

"I need to go now."

The statement shattered the man's heart, still wishing he didn't have to go and that they could go on pretending for just a little while longer.

"I'll come back."

The promise broke him apart wider and he closed his eyes as his tears betrayed him, "I know."

"*Freeze!*"

Every Single Kiss

"I'll be right here when you come out." Dean promised, kissing the raven-haired man's hand. Cas' crystal blue eyes were pleading--he looked so forlorn lying in the hospital bed waiting for the nurses to come and take him away. Of course, he would be there when he got out. It wouldn't even be that long, it was only his tonsils.

"What if I don't?" Cas chewed his lip nervously.

"What if you don't...?"

"Come out."

"Cas, you'll be fine. It's nothing to worry about."

"Then you do it."

Dean chuckled and shook his head. Whenever he was scared, he always acted like a five-year-old.

"We need to take him in now," a nurse interrupted from the door.

"Dean, please, I don't want to go," Cas panicked as more nurses walked into his room.

"C'mon, Cas-"

"Dean, *please*. Can't we just go home?" He gripped the blonde's hand tighter and turned puppy dog eyes on him.

"Cas, it's all right. You'll be okay. I promise. We can go home after you come out of surgery," Dean disentangled his hand with care.

Cas looked like someone had just shot his dog and it was hard for Dean to see him so scared. He was supposed to protect and keep him safe, not cause him pain.

But you're not *causing him pain. For God's sake it's just some tonsils. He's acting like they're removing his brain. Kids have this surgery and never flip out. Even if it is his first surgery, it's no reason to act like a crazy person.*

One of the nurses approached the bed carrying an I.V. much to Cas' distress. "Dean!" Cas' panicked voice shot straight through his heart.

Stupid feelings.

Evading the squirming patient, the nurse got the I.V. in without any fuss and applied tape to keep it from moving. Cas looked down to the needle sticking out of the back of his hand, his eyes wounded. "She stabbed me," he looked up at Dean in confusion, his bottom lip quivering. "Why did she stab me?"

Dean chuckled, but not unkindly, "She didn't stab you, Sweetpea. They're just getting you ready. It's just the I.V."

Two more nurses approached and pulled up the bed rails from either side, getting him ready to move and raising Cas' trepidation.

"Cas, I can one-hundred percent guarantee that nothing will happen to you. It's a simple surgery, I'm sure the doctor could do it blindfolded," Dean raised an eyebrow at the nurses, silently asking them to help.

"Oh yeah, don't worry. Doc's been doing this for years. In fact, I think I even overheard him mention needing a blindfold to one of the surgical nurses," the nurse, Jim, replied with a wink.

"*Dean.*"

"No-no-no, Cas, c'mon, he's just kidding." Dean shot the guy a cold glare.

"He's ready," one of the other nurses said.

"Okay babe, I'll see you when you get back," Dean pressed a goodbye kiss to his forehead.

"You're not coming with me?" His voice trembled, eyes as big as when Gabriel told him Santa wasn't real.

"No, buddy, I'm not allowed in the operating room," Dean explained softly.

"You could watch in the observation room above the surgery if you wanted," Jim suggested.

"Yes," Cas nodded his head vigorously. "The observation room."

"Okay, then, I guess I can come."

Cas visibly relaxed, but still reached for Dean's hand and jumped a bit when they started wheeling him out to the hall.

"How long will it take?" Cas' eyes never moved off the blonde walking beside them.

"Shouldn't take too long."

"So I can come home tonight?"

"I think so. They might want to keep you overnight, though. Just to make sure you're okay," Dean said with a shrug.

"I might not be okay?"

"No, it's just... kids get this surgery all the time and it's nothing, like twenty minutes tops. You're a grown-up, is all. Might take more out of you. Just guessing," Dean wondered why none of the nurses bothered jumping in.

"Oh..."

Cas kissed his hand as they arrived at the big double doors.

"Will it hurt?" Cas' voice was laced with sudden urgency.

"Not even a little. They'll knock you out. You won't even remember it happened. And when you wake up, I'll bring you a popsicle," he gave him a wink.

"To get to the observation room, you just need to go up through there," Jim point to a stairwell off to the right.

"Okay, thanks."

"I guess this is it," Cas' voice was small.

"You'll be okay. I promise," Dean repeated, wishing he could make that scared look go away.

"I love you."

"I love you too, Sweetpea," Dean blew him a kiss as they wheeled him in.

He went up to the observation room and immediately looked down, seeing Cas' bed parked beside a metal table. They were already knocking him out and Dean tried to hold in a chuckle as Cas' eyes immediately flew up to the giant window where he was standing. He gave the man a little wave and a thumbs up before his eyes fluttered closed.

Dean ran a hand through his hair and turned around, this time taking a good look at the observation room. There wasn't much too it--a couple screens to the right of the window showed vitals and what he guessed was some other important medical crap, a weird metal box with a speaker in it underneath that, an office chair, a little wooden table against the opposite wall and a vent.

Guess no one ever gets bored watching these, he twirled around in the chair a few times. *I wonder what the window's made out of...*

He scooted himself closer and gave it a light tap. To his surprise it sounded like glass.

"If you're trying to break it, you'll need a lot more force," a voice from behind him offered.

He spun the chair around to see a young woman standing in the doorway with a smirk on her face.

"Thanks for the tip," he replied cautiously as he came to his feet.

"I'm going out on a limb here and guess you're Dean and not the escaped patient from our ward on three?" She asked, walking over to shake his hand.

"Oh, I wouldn't be making assumptions like that, Sister. I could be crazy," Dean replied with a smirk, taking her hand.

"Crazy, I believe, but not too bright it seems," she countered with her own smile.

"Oh?" He sat back down and crossed his arms. "You don't say?"

"I never said it was the psyche ward."

"Oh."

"I'm Hannah, by the way. The attending physician." The red-head walked past him to the window, taking in the operating theatre below.

"Riiight..." Dean also turning back to the surgery, "And how often do tonsillectomies go wrong again?"

"Not as often as heart surgeries. Much less than appendectomies," she said with assurance.

"But often enough they need an attending?" His face reflected his skepticism and he shot her a glance from under a lowered brow.

"I oversee all surgeries. Don't worry, we didn't give your friend to a med student," she smiled.

"No?"

"They would never work alone even if we did. In this instance, quite the opposite, actually. By luck of rotation, one of our best surgeons is rooting around in your friend there, so he's in good hands."

"Oh well, when you put it like *that*," Dean rolled his eyes.

"Somehow, I read you the type not to be offended by a description like that," she pronounced with a sly smile.

Dean watched the activity below for a few minutes in silence. Not much was going on that he could see. "So..," he inhaled deeply and stretched, "basically you're on a break when you're in here?"

"Basically."

Dean chuckled and shook his head--at least Cas would be happy knowing one of the best surgeons had worked on him. It wasn't only four nurses and a highly trained surgeon, but *also* an overseeing physician making sure nothing went wrong. It's like they knew it was his first surgery and they were doing everything they could to prevent him from having a bad experience. It was basically the five-star dining experience of hospitals.

"Do you always do that or just when you're bored?" Hannah was examining him with an amused expression on her face.

"Do what?" Dean looked confused.

"Narrate what you're thinking."

"Shit, I said that out loud?" His cheeks turned red.

"Yep," she nodded with a laugh and leaned a hip against the window. "You sticking around? You're the best time I've had all day."

"Sorry. I didn't mean for that to be, uh, shared with the class," Dean mumbled, crossing his arms over his chest.

"No, it's fine. I found it charming."

Oh great...

They fell into a comfortable silence--or at least he *hoped* they did, now that he knew he'd apparently been narrating--and turned back to the surgery. Dean stood up and got closer to the window. His back stiffened.

Something was definitely wrong.

The surgeon was covered in way too much blood for a tonsillectomy and one of the nurses was holding several gauze pads at the ready, looking surprised. A surgical tray held several more stained red.

"What happened?" His voice tight, his eyes flicked back up to Hannah, but she didn't answer. Because she wasn't beside him any longer.

He turned from the window to find her gone and took a few charged steps in her direction until he realized she was on the phone.

When did that happen?

"What's going on?" Dean held her eyes, torn between getting an answer from her and keeping watch over the sudden frantic activity over Cas' unconscious form.

She held up a finger to silence him and pressed the receiver closer to her ear, knuckles turning white with redirected energy, though to her credit, she kept any anxiety from her expression. Dean could feel his heart leap into his throat and it was a lifetime before she finally hung up.

"So?"

"They think they nicked something. Maybe. And the anaesthesia's wearing off," she relayed, her tone professional and supportive. She made a calming gesture with both her hands, "They're putting him back under now. Don't worry, they're getting the situation under control."

"He nicked something?" Dean asked in confusion.

"Possibly. They're not certain. There were unexpected complications."

"But… It was just tonsils. *You* said he was one of your best."

"Yes, I did say that. And that's still true." Hannah was speaking quickly, working to bring Dean into focus, "He is. And he's the best person for your friend in this moment. More important, right now? You focus on our getting the situation under control. Can you do that for me?"

Strained with concern, Dean dipped his head in response. "Boyfriend."

"I'm sorry?"

A long moment passed before he spoke again, working to process what was happening. "He's my boyfriend."

While strained, her eyes conveyed that she understood the emotional connection. Her voice softened slightly, "Okay. Let me get a handle on what's going on for you. Can you sit tight here for me?"

He nodded mutely.

"Good. I want you to stay right here. I need to get down there before-"

She was cut off by raised voices from below, "Hold him down before he pulls out the I.V.!" and the loud crash of a surgical tray hitting the floor. Dean jerked back to the window to witness Cas' twitching, *twitching?!* body, his back arched unnaturally off the table.

"Oh, great," Hannah mumbled, sounding more disappointed than anything else.

"Cas!" Dean pounded a useless fist against the window.

Down below him, the anaesthesiologist readjusted the face mask before administering more sedative through the I.V., working fast while the nurses wrestled Cas to keep him still.

Damn it Cas, let them help!

"Why's he fighting them?" He asked of a no-longer-there Hannah.

Shit.

Frustrated, he paced, not sure how to help, but his body compelling him to jump in and save his love. He saw Hannah burst in on the surgical team, a hastily pulled-on gown and mask in place, but her unscrubbed arms held up out of the way of touching anything. She barked orders, everyone freezing momentarily to listen.

With a definitive nod, the team re-animated, the anaesthesiologist checking Cas' vitals while a nurse held gauze out to the surgeon who was already working again to stop the bleeding. A nurse rushed out of the room while another stood in the corner talking at a furious pace with Hannah.

"Dean?" A female voice from behind him made him jump.

"What happened?"

The nurse leaned in through the half-open door. "Our attending, Doctor Smith, wanted me to let you know the surgeon is stitching him up now and you'll be able to sit with Castiel in the recovery room once they're finished."

"Thanks." Dean didn't appreciate the way his questions kept being side-stepped. "You were in the there. Can you tell me what happened? Please. Is he going to be all right?"

The nurse answered with a generic, "The surgeon has the situation under control. Nothing you need to worry about," before disappearing again.

Are they all allergic to giving straight answers? Dean plopped himself down in the chair and ground his teeth in frustration.

"Cas!" Dean exclaimed, jumping to his feet, heart back in his throat as he saw two of the nurses wheel over a crash cart.

He stood watching in horror as they shocked the shorter man, holding his breath and begging him to breathe. They shocked him again and that's when he felt his feet move under him, scenery whizzing past in a blur until he burst through the giant double doors and into the operating room.

"Cas!" He only got two steps before Jim put himself between Dean and the operating table.

"You can't be in here," he told Dean in a firm voice, herding him back toward the double doors with deliberate movements.

"Why isn't he breathing? What did you do to him?"

"Get him out of here!" The surgeon yelled from the other side of the room before shocking Cas' body again.

C'mon Cas… breathe damn it! Despite the rather large nurse forcing him out of the room, he refused, digging his heels in and unable to take his eyes off Cas' body. He was pushed back further anyway.

"You'll need to remain in the waiting room until the surgery's ended," Jim pointed down a corridor.

"What did you do to him?" Dean demanded.

"*Sir*, I need you to go to the waiting room. Someone will be out to explain everything as soon as possible," Jim balked at his rage, but didn't budge.

"I'm not going anywhere until you tell me what happened!" He punched the wall for emphasis making the surgical team jump.

"You're distracting the surgical team. If you care about your friend, you'll let them do their jobs. Do you understand?" Jim was understanding, but firm, "Don't make me call security, Sir."

Dean sighed and ran a shaking hand down his face. With an arching last look over Jim's shoulder to the table behind him, Dean forced himself out the doors. Numb, he trudged off in the direction of the waiting room.

Don't you die on me.

*****

"Dean?"

At the mention of his name, his head whipped up and he was standing in front of Hannah before he realized he was vertical.

"Is he..? What happened?" A tumble of words forced themselves past his lips, "Why isn't anyone telling me anything? I thought you said he was the best. This is the best you've got? How did he screw up tonsils? Clearly, you should start looking for a new best surgeon. What would have happened if you weren't overseeing that procedure? You better have some good news for me, Sister."

"Whoa, slow down there, Tiger," she said with a small smile.

"Sorry," he took a breath. "I guess I'm just a little anxious, because I watched you *reviving* him." Dean crossed his arms over his chest. He looked at her closely, "Well, you don't have your falsely sympathetic yet aloof face on, so it can't be all bad. So... you didn't kill him?"

"No, we didn't. A little worse for wear maybe, but he's fine," raising an eyebrow as if expecting him to protest. "The surgeon *did* nick something, the interior carotid artery to be precise. But that was an accident. Your boyfriend suffered a TIA, a Transient Ischemic Attack, while under anaesthesia. That's a mini stroke. That's what was happening when you saw him twitching. It was sudden. There's no way to predict that would happen. It was during that episode the artery was nicked-"

"Wait, what? Cas had a stroke?" Dean closed his eyes momentarily and ran his hands up into his hair. "How does that even happen?" He took a deep breath and dropped his hands. "Okay, sorry, go on."

"It's all right. It's a lot to take in. The most important thing is he's stable now. There's no more bleeding. And his tonsils are gone," she gave him a small smile.

"I guess mission accomplished then," his voice was dark with sarcasm.

Hannah let him have that one and didn't comment. "The TIA is a bit more serious, though. Doesn't necessarily mean that he'll have an actual stroke in the future and this was a warning, but we'll consider him at risk for a full stroke within the next several months. To be sure he's clear, we need to find the cause. Then we'll know how to proceed. Could have been a single instance and the small clot that caused it will dissolve on its own and then no more problem. At worst, we may discover he has Atherosclerosis, hardening of the arteries, which could have been the source of the clot, but we can give him medication for that. We just need to find out."

"That's uh..," Dean's face was strained. "Wow. Okay, so I'm guessing you'll want to keep him overnight, at least?"

"Yes, at least for tonight. As I said, we'll know more after we get the test results."

Dean felt his knees weaken as the threat level went down several notches. He placed a hand on the wall to steady himself. "C-can I see him?" His voice as shaky as his legs felt.

"He's not awake yet, but you can sit with him in the recovery room," Hannah smiled, pointing the way.

"Thanks."

It didn't feel like he ran down the hall, but it seemed possible since in a blink of an eye he was suddenly standing outside the recovery ward doorway. He took a deep breath before going in.

"Cas?" He kept his voice low as he walked over to the bed.

The shorter man didn't look too worse for wear, and he was definitely a sight for sore eyes. Being so close to him after the forced distance was surreal--in that moment, watching over his sleeping form, it became very evident how much his life was tangled up with this beautiful human being. He trailed his hand down along his arm, pausing at the hospital tag, before slipping his hand into Cas' limp one, no longer able to remain detached from the other half of his heart. He hooked a chair over with his foot, plopping himself as close to the bed as he could.

"You rest, my angel. I'll be here when you wake up," Dean whispered, pressing a kiss to his forehead.

Some time later, he jumped awake at the feel of something squeezing his hand. He rubbed his eyes and looked around, the scenery taking a minute to compute with his tired brain.

"D'n?"

It was absurdly exciting to hear his voice, however slurred.

"Yeah, Cas, I'm right here."

Cas' eyes blinked open slowly, squinting and turning his head against the bright lights. He looked up to the blonde standing over him and a small smile appeared on his face, body visibly relaxing to see his boyfriend.

He smoothed a lock of hair off his forehead, "You okay, Cas?" Dean couldn't help but ask, wrapping him up in a hug.

"I'm fine," his voice was hushed and scratchy, but it didn't matter. He wrapped his arms around Dean's shoulders. "You look so worried. What happened?" Still a bit groggy, Cas let go and dropped his arms back down to his lap.

Dean took a couple steps back and barked out a laugh-- what *didn't* happen was a much better question. "We can talk about it in a while, Sweetpea. You should rest your throat."

"Okay fine," he whispered. "First, tell me what *didn't* happen," Cas blinked up at the taller man with expectation.

Damn my out loud narration! Dean mentally kicked himself.

"Dean?" Worry crept into his voice.

"It's nothing, Cas."

"Dean..," he warned.

"Okay, okay... Let's just say? I now share your fear of hospitals."

Love Island

"Hi, welcome to Love Island." The hostess greeted the pair with a thousand-watt grin as they reached the front doors of the resort. "We hope you enjoy your stay!"

"Thanks!" Luce side-stepped her with the agility of gazelle and darted away, sprinting across the lobby.

"Luce," Sam spoke to his back with a smile, "will you calm down?"

"Calm down? Are you kidding? Did you *not* hear?" He reached the elevator and pressed the button incessantly while he panted. "Free. Complimentary. All-day. *Breakfast!*"

Sam laughed and worked to hold down his arm before he wore out the elevator call button, "Yeah, so?" Sam could barely contain the vibrating blonde.

"I looked them up online," he ran into the elevator as the doors opened.

"And...?" Sam followed him in.

"Poptarts, Sammy! They have Poptarts!" Luce shouted triumphantly as the elevator doors closed.

*****

"Luce," Sam called after the man bouncing down the hallway. "Slow down, Luce!" Sam was still struggling to catch up as he disappeared into one of the rooms.

Sam finally got to the door and turned the knob. It was locked, *Of course.* He knocked. "Can you let me in? It's locked, " he called through, shifting one of the bags on his shoulder. "Luce, c'mon, this stuff is heavy," Sam called again after a moment of silence.

Maybe this isn't the right room… He took a step back away from the door and looked up and down the hallway. *Well I can't exactly play ding-dong ditch with all rooms until I find him,* He dropped one of the bags beside him. "Luce!" Sam raised his voice, searching each door up and down the hall. And starting to get annoyed.

"Sammy! What're you doing standing out in the hall?" The shorter man poked his head out the door and beckoned, "Get in here."

"Didn't you hear me?" Sam picked the bag back up and walked passed him into the room.

"Nope," Luce closed the door behind him.

"Of course not," the giant mumbled and dropped the bags. A second later he grabbed hold of the shorter man.

"Whoa! Sam wh-"

Sam purred in his ear, "I had a whole plane ride to think about what I was going to do to you once I got you alone," nibbling on it gently.

"Y-yeah?" Luce asked breathlessly, knees going weak.

"Oh yeah," the taller man smirked and pushed him down onto the bed.

"Is it anything good?" Luce flushed with excitement.

"Trust me," Sam raked hungry eyes over him, "you'll love it."

*****

Luce was panting, curled up beside the giant.

"Told you," Sam smirked, kissing the top of his forehead.

"That was… Oh, my God," evidently he was at a loss for words.

"I know," Sam chuckled, bringing the sleepy man closer to his chest.

"What was the occasion for that?" Luce snuggled his head against him.

"Well, we're here to celebrate Valentine's Day and I thought, what better way to start the trip than with a little love?"

"We're going to do that again, right?" Luce closed his eyes.

"We're here for the whole weekend. We're going to be doing a *lot* more of that," Sam smirked.

"I might need a nap first," Luce slurred.

"Yes, yes you will."

*****

Luce rolled over and looked at the clock: 9:30am.

*No…*He rolled back toward his giant, reaching his arm over to cuddle. "S'm?" His arm fell onto bedding instead of onto naked man.

He listened carefully for his lover, but was only greeted by silence. "Sam?" He popped his head up and rubbed at his eyes. There was only more silence. Luce frowned and scanned the darkened room for the brunette.

Where did he go? Curiosity pulled him out of bed.

"Oohh…" He cooed, feeling the plush white carpet under his bare feet. "Nice." He continued farther into the room which held a disturbing lack of naked giant. He reached the bathroom and there was still no sign of his boyfriend.

Where are you? Luce leaned into the shower and turned the water on. Waiting on the water to warm up, he scanned the luxurious room. The website was right, they definitely went all out for Valentine's Day--their soap was carved into hearts, red towels covered in hearts and even the bathmat was the shape of a heart. *Sammy... How far could you have gone? You're naked... And missing... My boyfriend is naked and missing on Valentine's.*

He stepped into the shower and closed the door, sighing in relief as the warm water hit his body. He leaned on his hands against the wall and dropped his head, allowing the water to run down his back, relaxing his muscles. He closed his eyes and shifted ever-so-slightly, allowing it to flow down over his sore neck.

Luce chuckled, *Damn his aggressiveness...*

Hands came up his back and massaged his shoulders, relaxing him further.

Wait a minute... Luce's head shot up, spraying water all over the place.

"Whoa, whoa," Sam whispered, "it's just me." Sam snaked his hands down over Luce's chest.

"Where'd you go?" Luce lowered his head again and let himself relax at the touch.

"I was planning a little somethin'-somethin'," he smirked, continuing to massage down the blonde's front.

"Oh, yeah?" Luce broke out into goose bumps.

"Oh, yeah."

"Do I get to know or...?" He trailed off, feeling the giant's hand reach his dick.

"That depends..," Sam breathed, keeping his hand agonizingly close, but not touching.

"On?"

"Is this for me?"

Luce nodded his head and let out a little moan, feeling his hand wrap around the head. The shorter man lazily rolled his hips forward against the giant's hand as he rubbed it, trying to gain more friction.

"Don't tell me you want some more already?" Sam chuckled against his ear.

"I *always* want more," Luce countered with his own smile.

"That's true," Sam dragged his hand up his shaft slowly.

"Ohhh…" Luce cooed, unconsciously leaning his head back against the giant's chest.

"You liking this?" Sam asked in a hushed tone, tugging twice against his tip before pulling his hand away.

"You're killin' me," Luce breathed, groaning at the sudden lack of contact.

"Good."

Before he knew it, Luce was spun around to face his giant with his back pressed against the opposite wall. Sam dropped to his knees and took his length into his mouth.

"Oh, my God!" Luce exclaimed, resting a hand on the back of his head.

Sam bobbed up and down his dick a couple times before pulling it out with a smirk.

"So horny for me," Sam cooed, staying on his knees, wrapping a hand back around his dick.

Luce moaned, but otherwise didn't answer, too lost in the pleasure to coherently string a sentence together. Sam's other hand started massaging up and down his legs and it wasn't until he smelled something fruity that he opened his eyes.

"What is that?" Luce glanced down at the giant who was washing him.

"Strawberry body wash," Sam took his other hand off his dick to rub some together and do the other leg.

"It smells good," Luce sniffed the air.

Sam chuckled, washing back up to his torso.

Luce let out another little moan as the giant 'accidentally' brushed his leg against his dick as he stood back up. Sam continued to wash the shorter man in silence, concentrating on making contact with every inch of his skin and Luce loving how relaxing it was to feel his hands. Luce opened his eyes to watch as Sam took the shower head out of its holder and brought it closer to carefully rinse off his lover's body.

"Damn you're good at this," weak in the knees, Luce was glad he was still against the wall.

"It's not my first time," Sam rinsed up his arms.

"No, it is not," Luce sighed.

Sam chuckled and moved the showerhead up to his hair, thoroughly wetting it while he massaged the scalp underneath, sending another wave of goose bumps over the blonde. The giant put the shower head back before grabbing the shampoo and applying that to his hair, taking longer than necessary. He spun the shorter man back around, placing him once again under the spray and massaged/rinsed the shampoo out with careful attention.

"What about you?" Luce asked as he heard the water shut off.

"I already showered," Sam reached over and grabbed the towels.

"Well, you're already here..," Luce took the offered towel, "and you didn't shower with *me*..."

"No-no. Today is all about pleasing you," Sam pressed a kiss to his forehead.

"You being clean *would* please me," he countered with a smile.

"I've *never* been clean," Sam stepped out of the shower and threw the damp towel over the shower rail.

"You're going to walk around naked?" Luce stepped out and wrapped the towel around his waist.

"Trust me, with what I have planned? You won't be needing clothes."

Authors' Note

I don't think I could ever properly express just how excited I am that this is being published--it's crazy! I'd like to thank anyone who's reading this for supporting my writing, as without readers I'm basically talking into the void. Although since you'll all be reading this long after I've finished writing it, I kind of *am* talking into a void and just hoping there's someone on the other side…

This e-book was made in the hopes it'd be ready for Valentine's Day--hence the collection of slash fics. I didn't write all of these with the intention of putting them together in a collection, but as any writer knows, the stories tend to take on a life of their own halfway through.

I'm actually kind of surprised I wrote this many fluffy pieces--I think you can tell where my brain shattered and tried to get back on the right path of not so much fluff with 'Your Hearts A Liar!' But I think 'A Thousand Promises' and 'Love Island' makes up for the darkness of that fic. And, in case any of you are wondering, *yes*, that through-the-hedge scene in 'A Thousand Promises' has the mushiest/cutest proclamation of love I've ever written and I think writing it has altered my brain. (At least a little)

I'd like to permanently thank country artists for being able to write such great love songs as that's pretty much all I listened to when writing that fic and I'm like 80% certain I wouldn't have been able to do that without the outside help. Along the same lines, I'd also like to thank the two mushiest/most romantic people I know--you guys definitely had a hand in me being able to pull this off.

Also, in case anyone's wondering, the fics are listed in the order in which I wrote them--Sunday Blues being the oldest, while Love Island is the most 'current'.

I hope you guys enjoyed it and I'm looking forward to hearing what you think.

AI

Acknowledgements and Credits

A Thousand Promises:

- Gabriel sings 'I wish I could carry your smile in my heart' - line taken from the song 'All Out Of Love' by Air Supply

Album 'Lost In Love' Copyright: 1980 Arista Records Inc., song written by Graham Russell and Clive Davis

Special thanks to J.D Stanley for helping me with the editing.

About the Author

Ater Imber became interested in writing fan fiction in 2013 after being talked into giving the DeviantArt website a chance. Ater began posting to the delight of Supernatural fans and continues to write new fan fiction stories with regularity for an eager personal following.

Ater's debut fan fiction novella, *Don't Get Caught*, a collection of short stories based upon the t.v. series Supernatural, published on the Kobo platform in February 2016.

Ater continues to maintain a presence on DA (http://aterimber.deviantart.com/), an additional home on Archive of Our Own (http://archiveofourown.org/users/aterimber), Wattpad (https://www.wattpad.com/user/AterImber) and several social media accounts including Twitter (@AterImber), Instagram (https://www.instagram.com/aterimber/) and Tumblr (http://aterimber.tumblr.com/).

Ater Imber lives in Toronto, Canada.

Printed in Poland
by Amazon Fulfillment
Poland Sp. z o.o., Wrocław